P9-APA-387

SUMMARY OF *THE SPACE RACE OF 1869*

The kingdom of Bavaria has been gripped by a strange restlessness.

The enigmatic King Ludwig has a secret ambition: to construct a revolutionary flying machine.

After discovering the logbooks of Claire Dulac, pioneering explorer of the celestial aether…

…he summons the husband of the vanished aethernaut and their son, Seraphin, to make his dreams a reality.

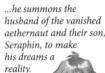

But he is not alone in his fascination with aether; others foresee disturbingly practical applications for it.

In fact, Bismarck, the formidable leader of Prussia, has planted an agent in Ludwig's castle…

> HOW INSIGNIFICANT ARE PETTY COLONIAL DISPUTES IN AFRICA WHEN VAST CONTINENTS LIE RIPE FOR CONQUEST ACROSS THE AETHER.

> IT'S *HIM!*

Hagen von Gudden, the king's own chamberlain!

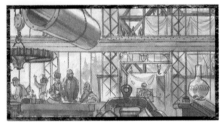

Professor Dulac will undertake the king's project: he will bring his wife's research to fruition by constructing an aethership that can travel through space and reach other worlds.

Meanwhile, Seraphin makes two friends at the castle: Hans and Sophie.

> WOW!

> GREAT! OKAY, SO NO ONE'S HERE! CAN WE LEAVE NOW?

> I'M SURE HE'LL LET ME COME ON BOARD, SOPHIE. EVERYTHING'S FUNCTIONING PROPERLY— NOTHING CAN GO WRONG!

The three children pledge to defend the king as the "Knights of Aether."

But when the dastardly von Gudden puts his plans into action…

> HAPPY ANNIVERSARY, YOUR MAJESTY.

…our heroes and the king narrowly escape on board the aethership.

Now, their own lives—as well as the fate of their research and the throne of Bavaria itself—depend on the success of this test flight…

> HANG ON!

ALEX ALICE

CASTLE
IN
THE
STARS

THE MOON-KING

First Second

New York

First Second

English translation by Anne and Owen Smith
English translation copyright © 2018 by Roaring Brook Press

Published by First Second
First Second is an imprint of Roaring Brook Press,
a division of Holtzbrinck Publishing Holdings Limited Partnership
175 Fifth Avenue, New York, NY 10010

Library of Congress Control Number: 2017915609

ISBN: 978-1-62672-494-5

Our books may be purchased in bulk for promotional, educational, or business use.
Please contact your local bookseller or the Macmillan Corporate and Premium Sales Department
at (800) 221-7945 ext. 5442 or by e-mail at MacmillanSpecialMarkets@macmillan.com.

Originally published in 2015 in French by Rue de Sèvres as *Le château des étoiles - 1869: La conquête de l'espace - Volume 2*
French text and illustrations by Alex Alice copyright © 2015 by Rue de Sèvres, Paris.
First American edition, 2018
Book design by Chris Dickey

Printed in China by RR Donnelley Asia Printing Solutions Ltd., Dongguan City, Guangdong Province
10 9 8 7 6 5 4 3 2

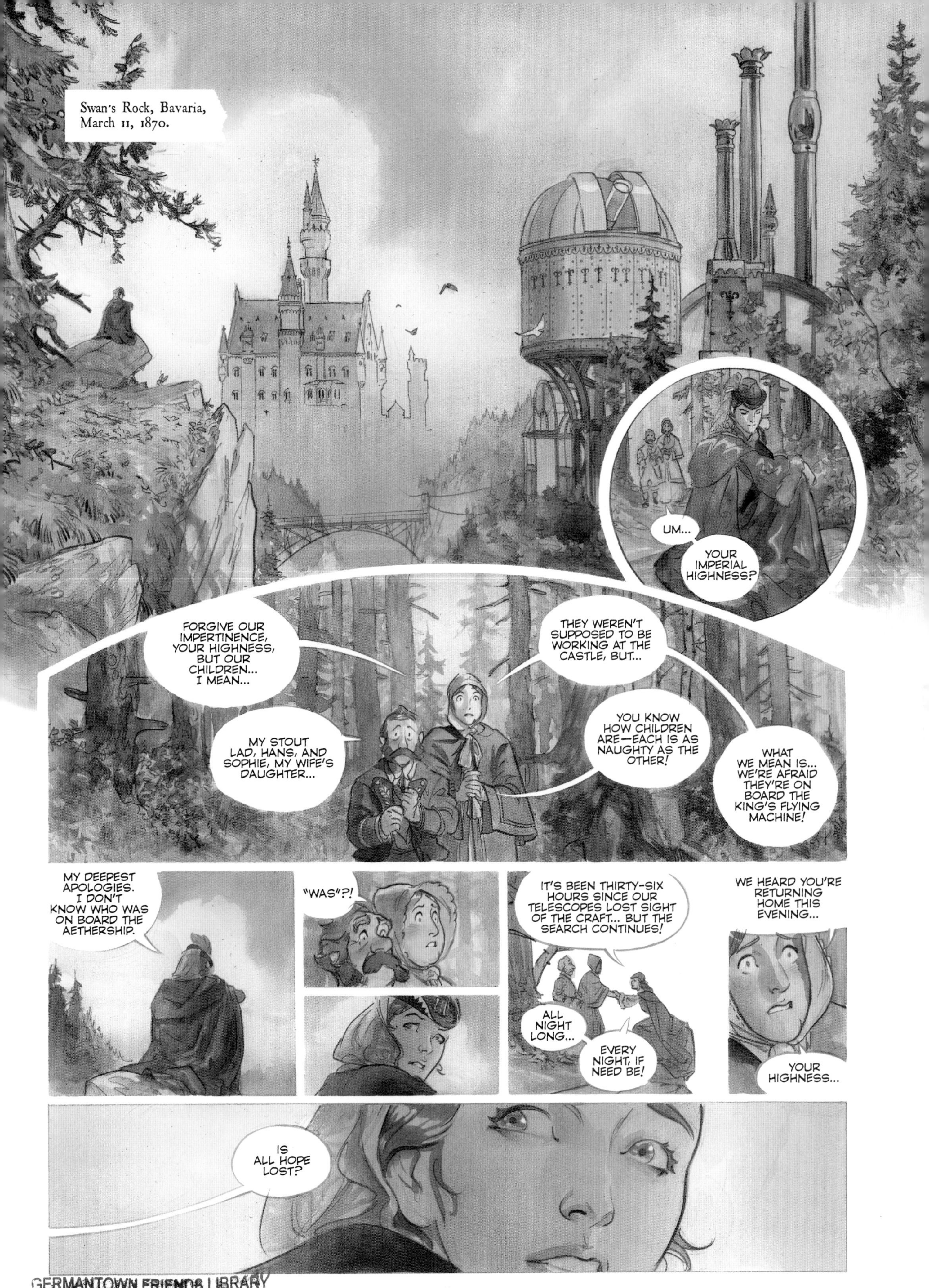
Swan's Rock, Bavaria,
March 11, 1870.
UM...
YOUR IMPERIAL HIGHNESS?
FORGIVE OUR IMPERTINENCE, YOUR HIGHNESS, BUT OUR CHILDREN... I MEAN...
THEY WEREN'T SUPPOSED TO BE WORKING AT THE CASTLE, BUT...
MY STOUT LAD, HANS, AND SOPHIE, MY WIFE'S DAUGHTER...
YOU KNOW HOW CHILDREN ARE—EACH IS AS NAUGHTY AS THE OTHER!
WHAT WE MEAN IS... WE'RE AFRAID THEY'RE ON BOARD THE KING'S FLYING MACHINE!
MY DEEPEST APOLOGIES. I DON'T KNOW WHO WAS ON BOARD THE AETHERSHIP.
"WAS"?!
IT'S BEEN THIRTY-SIX HOURS SINCE OUR TELESCOPES LOST SIGHT OF THE CRAFT... BUT THE SEARCH CONTINUES!
ALL NIGHT LONG...
EVERY NIGHT, IF NEED BE!
WE HEARD YOU'RE RETURNING HOME THIS EVENING...
YOUR HIGHNESS...
IS ALL HOPE LOST?

CHAPTER 4

SHIPWRECKED IN THE SKY

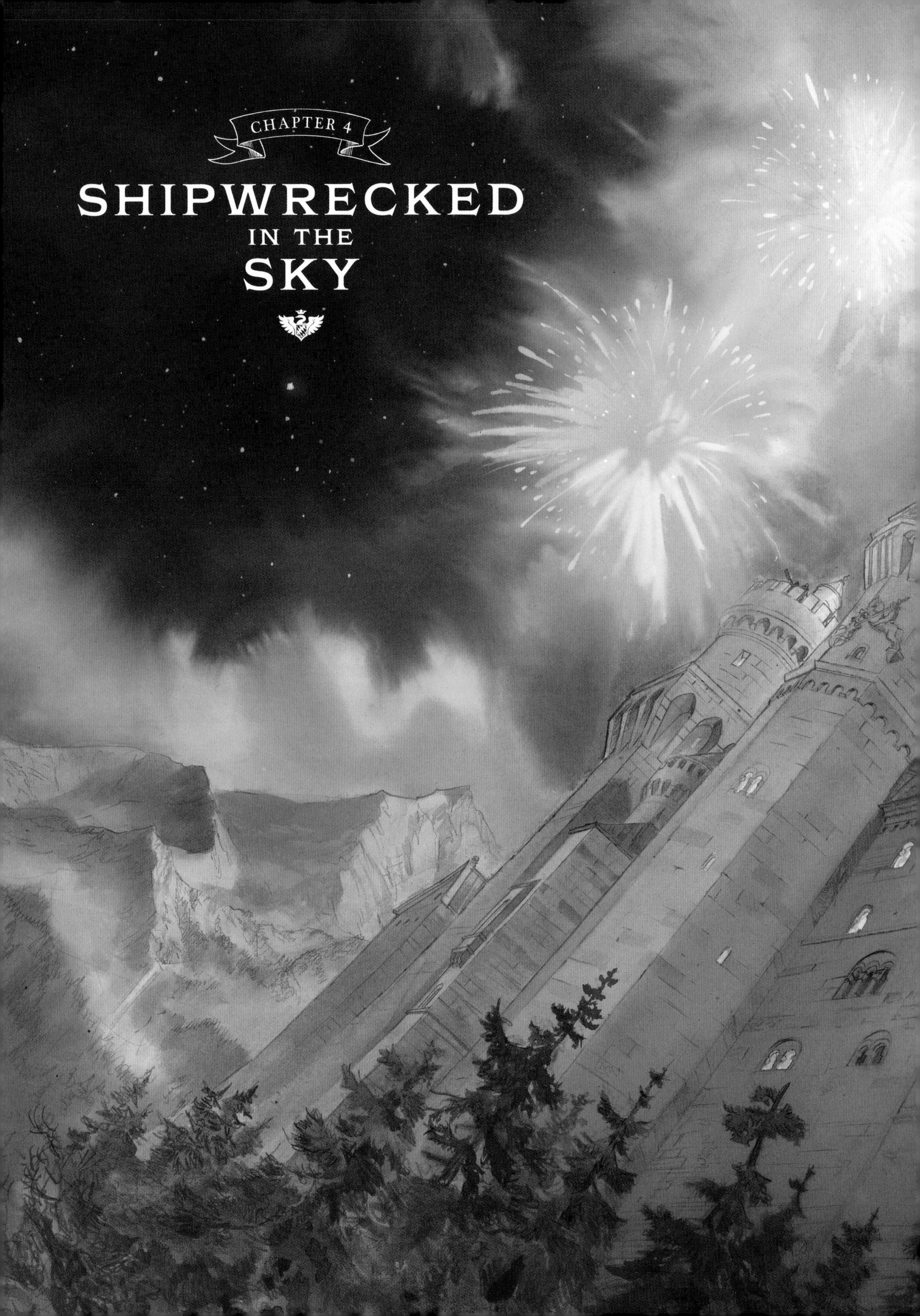

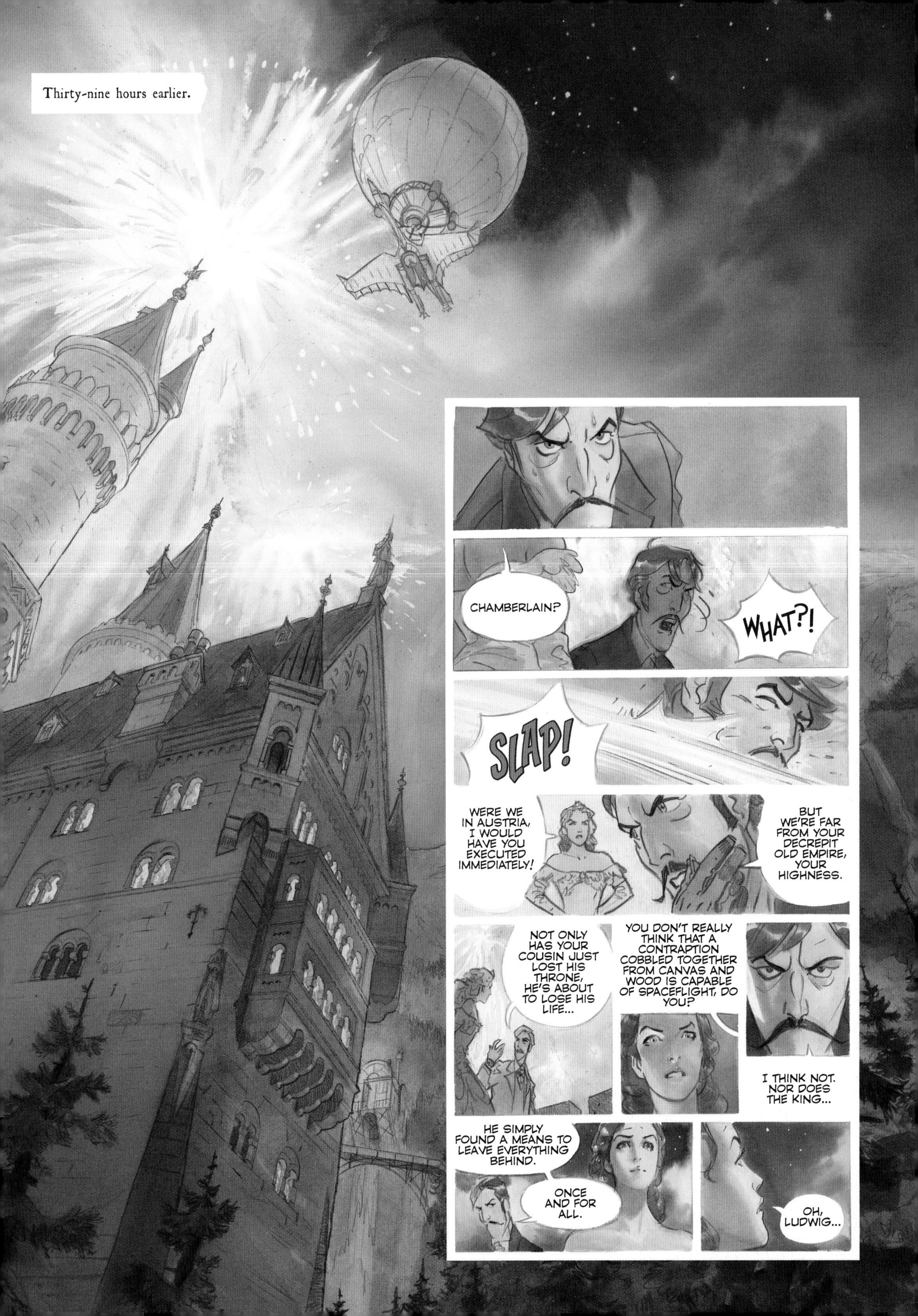
Thirty-nine hours earlier.
CHAMBERLAIN?
WHAT?!
SLAP!
WERE WE IN AUSTRIA, I WOULD HAVE YOU EXECUTED IMMEDIATELY!
BUT WE'RE FAR FROM YOUR DECREPIT OLD EMPIRE, YOUR HIGHNESS.
NOT ONLY HAS YOUR COUSIN JUST LOST HIS THRONE, HE'S ABOUT TO LOSE HIS LIFE...
YOU DON'T REALLY THINK THAT A CONTRAPTION COBBLED TOGETHER FROM CANVAS AND WOOD IS CAPABLE OF SPACEFLIGHT, DO YOU?
I THINK NOT. NOR DOES THE KING...
HE SIMPLY FOUND A MEANS TO LEAVE EVERYTHING BEHIND.
ONCE AND FOR ALL.
OH, LUDWIG...

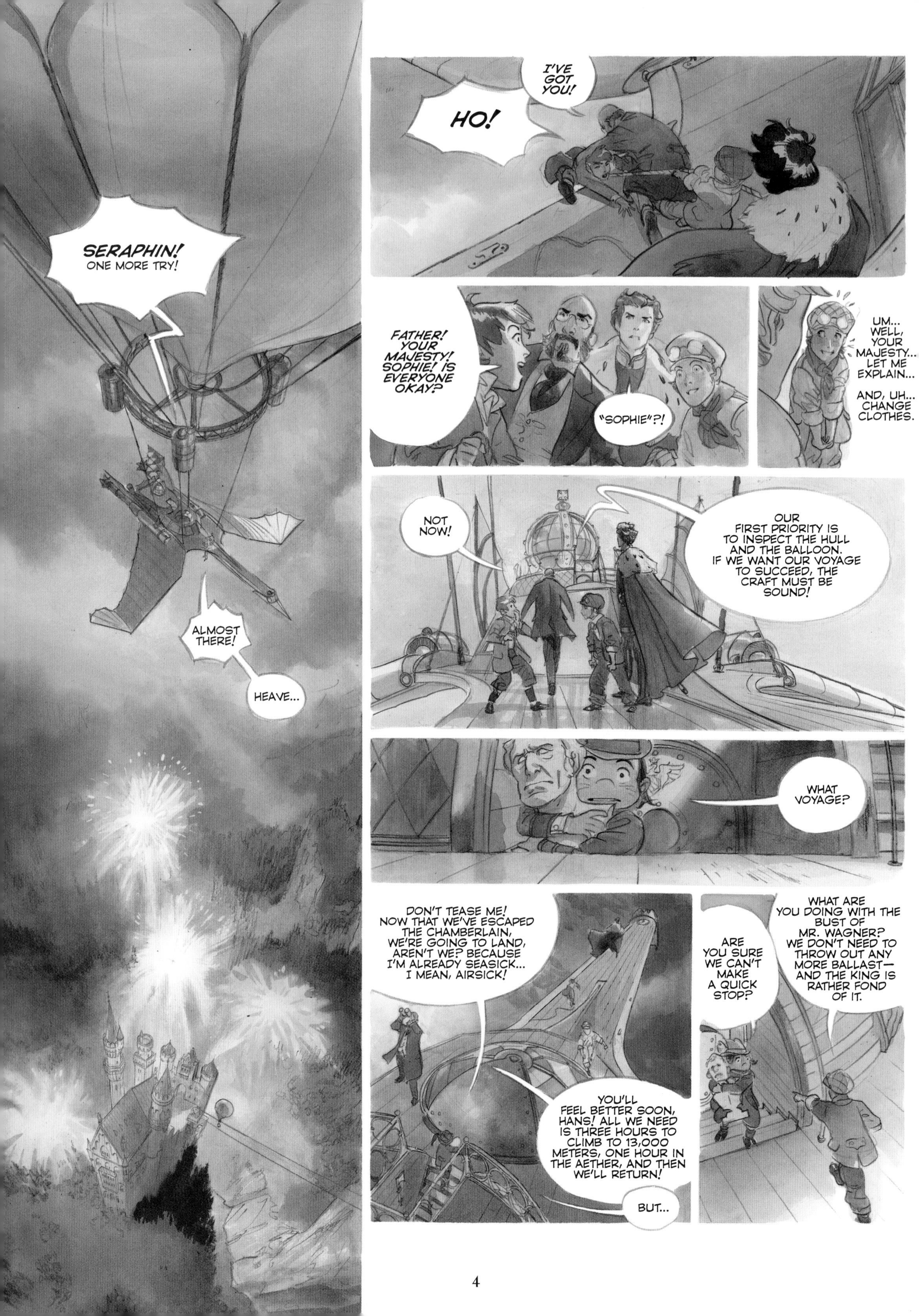
SERAPHIN! ONE MORE TRY!
ALMOST THERE!
HEAVE...
HO!
I'VE GOT YOU!
FATHER! YOUR MAJESTY! SOPHIE! IS EVERYONE OKAY?
"SOPHIE"?!
UM... WELL, YOUR MAJESTY... LET ME EXPLAIN...
AND, UH... CHANGE CLOTHES.
NOT NOW!
OUR FIRST PRIORITY IS TO INSPECT THE HULL AND THE BALLOON. IF WE WANT OUR VOYAGE TO SUCCEED, THE CRAFT MUST BE SOUND!
WHAT VOYAGE?
DON'T TEASE ME! NOW THAT WE'VE ESCAPED THE CHAMBERLAIN, WE'RE GOING TO LAND, AREN'T WE? BECAUSE I'M ALREADY SEASICK... I MEAN, AIRSICK!
YOU'LL FEEL BETTER SOON, HANS! ALL WE NEED IS THREE HOURS TO CLIMB TO 13,000 METERS, ONE HOUR IN THE AETHER, AND THEN WE'LL RETURN!
BUT...
ARE YOU SURE WE CAN'T MAKE A QUICK STOP?
WHAT ARE YOU DOING WITH THE BUST OF MR. WAGNER? WE DON'T NEED TO THROW OUT ANY MORE BALLAST—AND THE KING IS RATHER FOND OF IT.

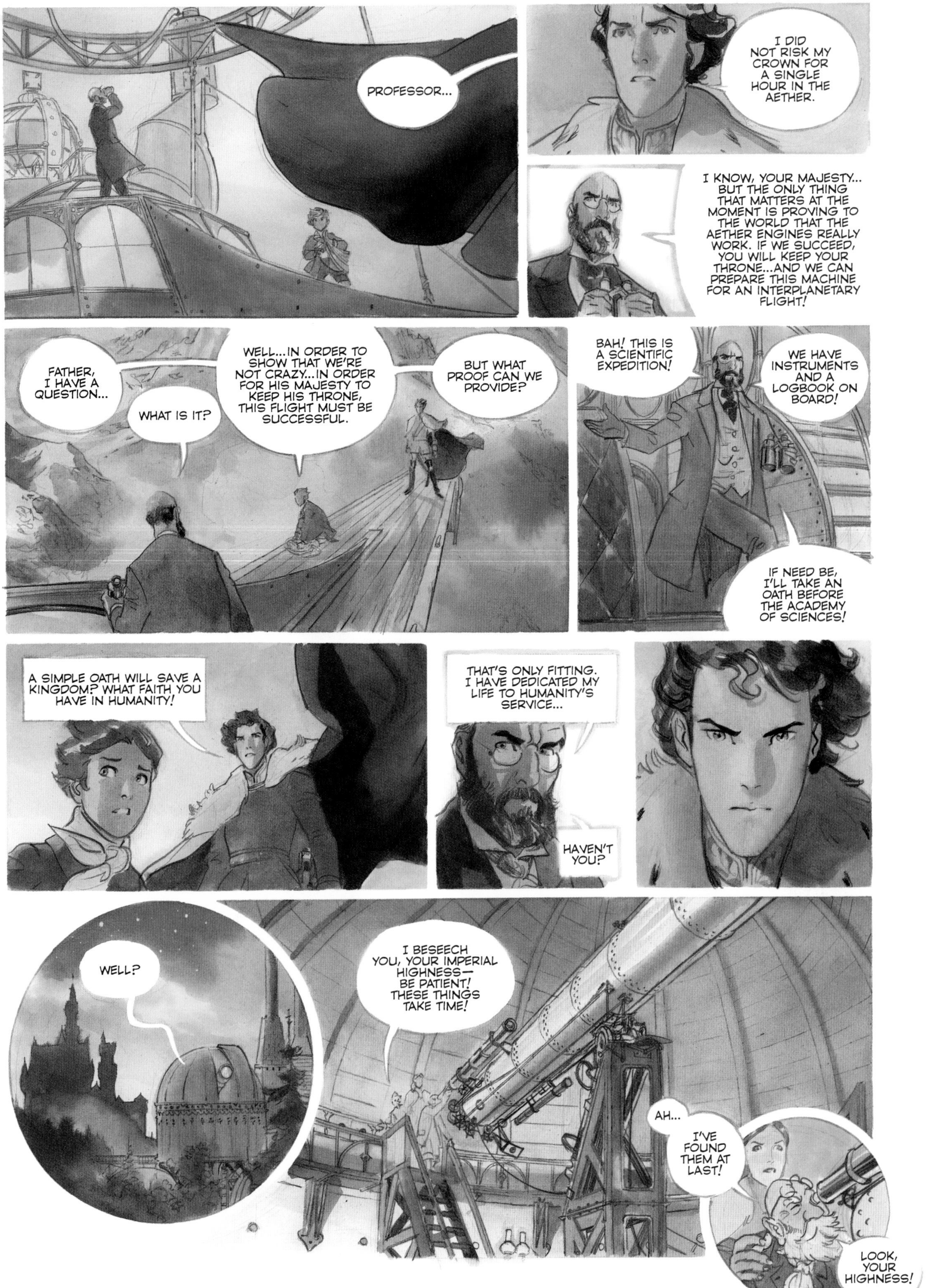
PROFESSOR...
I DID NOT RISK MY CROWN FOR A SINGLE HOUR IN THE AETHER.
I KNOW, YOUR MAJESTY... BUT THE ONLY THING THAT MATTERS AT THE MOMENT IS PROVING TO THE WORLD THAT THE AETHER ENGINES REALLY WORK. IF WE SUCCEED, YOU WILL KEEP YOUR THRONE...AND WE CAN PREPARE THIS MACHINE FOR AN INTERPLANETARY FLIGHT!
FATHER, I HAVE A QUESTION...
WHAT IS IT?
WELL...IN ORDER TO SHOW THAT WE'RE NOT CRAZY...IN ORDER FOR HIS MAJESTY TO KEEP HIS THRONE, THIS FLIGHT MUST BE SUCCESSFUL.
BUT WHAT PROOF CAN WE PROVIDE?
BAH! THIS IS A SCIENTIFIC EXPEDITION!
WE HAVE INSTRUMENTS AND A LOGBOOK ON BOARD!
IF NEED BE, I'LL TAKE AN OATH BEFORE THE ACADEMY OF SCIENCES!
A SIMPLE OATH WILL SAVE A KINGDOM? WHAT FAITH YOU HAVE IN HUMANITY!
THAT'S ONLY FITTING. I HAVE DEDICATED MY LIFE TO HUMANITY'S SERVICE...
HAVEN'T YOU?
WELL?
I BESEECH YOU, YOUR IMPERIAL HIGHNESS— BE PATIENT! THESE THINGS TAKE TIME!
AH...
I'VE FOUND THEM AT LAST!
LOOK, YOUR HIGHNESS!

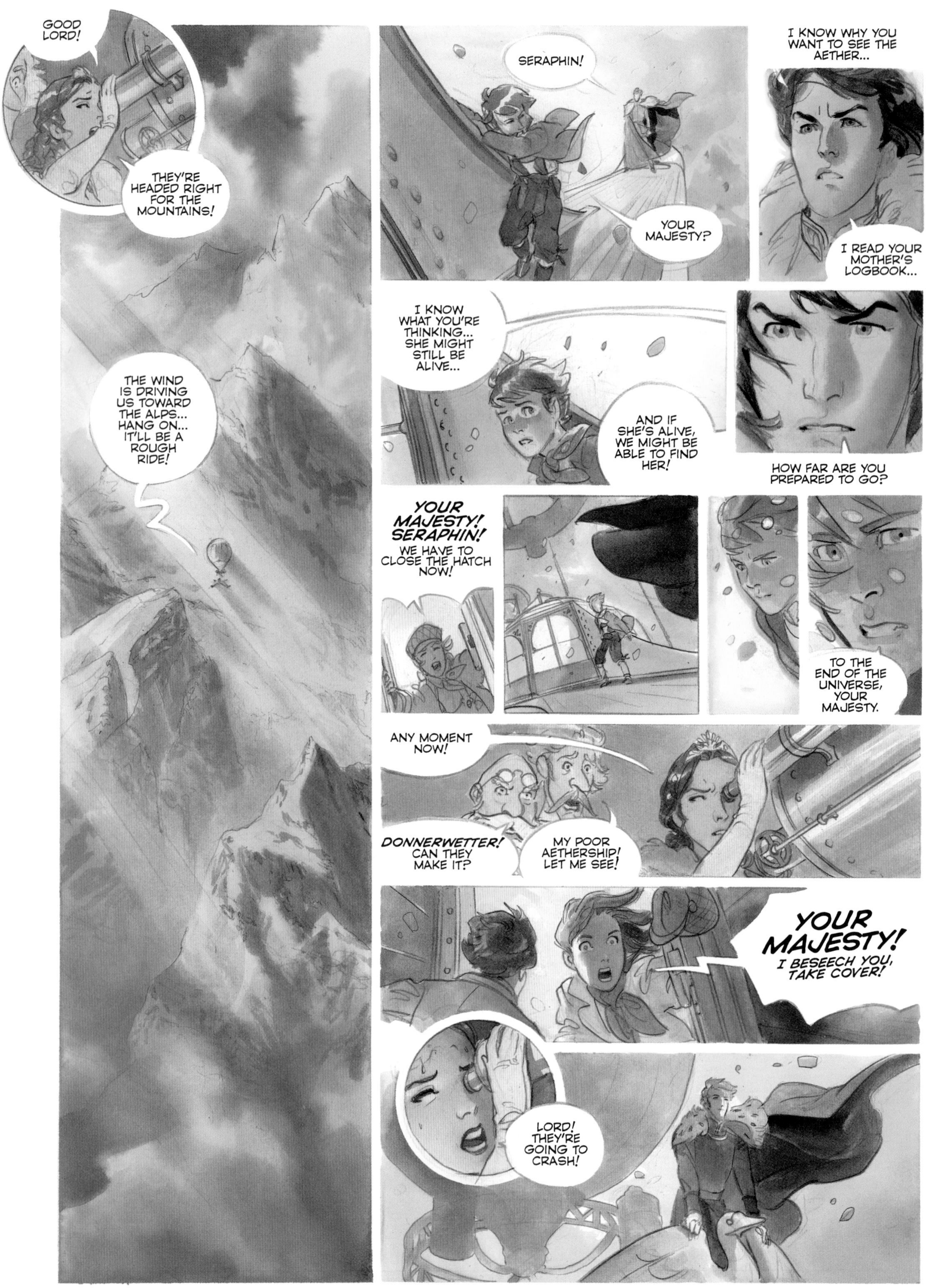
GOOD LORD!
THEY'RE HEADED RIGHT FOR THE MOUNTAINS!
THE WIND IS DRIVING US TOWARD THE ALPS... HANG ON... IT'LL BE A ROUGH RIDE!
SERAPHIN!
YOUR MAJESTY?
I KNOW WHY YOU WANT TO SEE THE AETHER...
I READ YOUR MOTHER'S LOGBOOK...
I KNOW WHAT YOU'RE THINKING... SHE MIGHT STILL BE ALIVE...
AND IF SHE'S ALIVE, WE MIGHT BE ABLE TO FIND HER!
HOW FAR ARE YOU PREPARED TO GO?
YOUR MAJESTY! SERAPHIN! WE HAVE TO CLOSE THE HATCH NOW!
TO THE END OF THE UNIVERSE, YOUR MAJESTY.
ANY MOMENT NOW!
DONNERWETTER! CAN THEY MAKE IT?
MY POOR AETHERSHIP! LET ME SEE!
YOUR MAJESTY! I BESEECH YOU, TAKE COVER!
LORD! THEY'RE GOING TO CRASH!

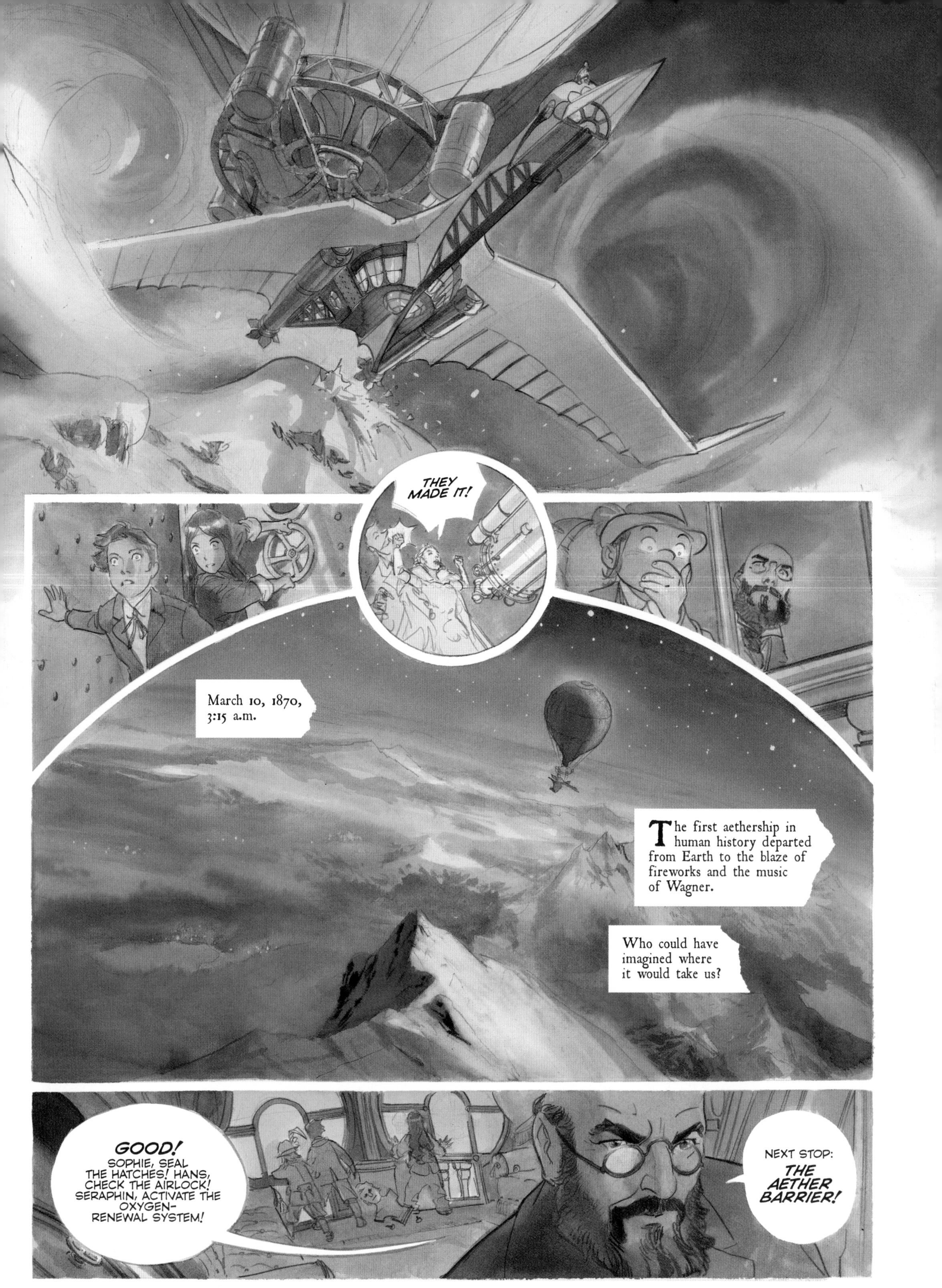

THEY MADE IT!
March 10, 1870, 3:15 a.m.
The first aethership in human history departed from Earth to the blaze of fireworks and the music of Wagner.
Who could have imagined where it would take us?
GOOD! SOPHIE, SEAL THE HATCHES! HANS, CHECK THE AIRLOCK! SERAPHIN, ACTIVATE THE OXYGEN-RENEWAL SYSTEM!
NEXT STOP: THE AETHER BARRIER!

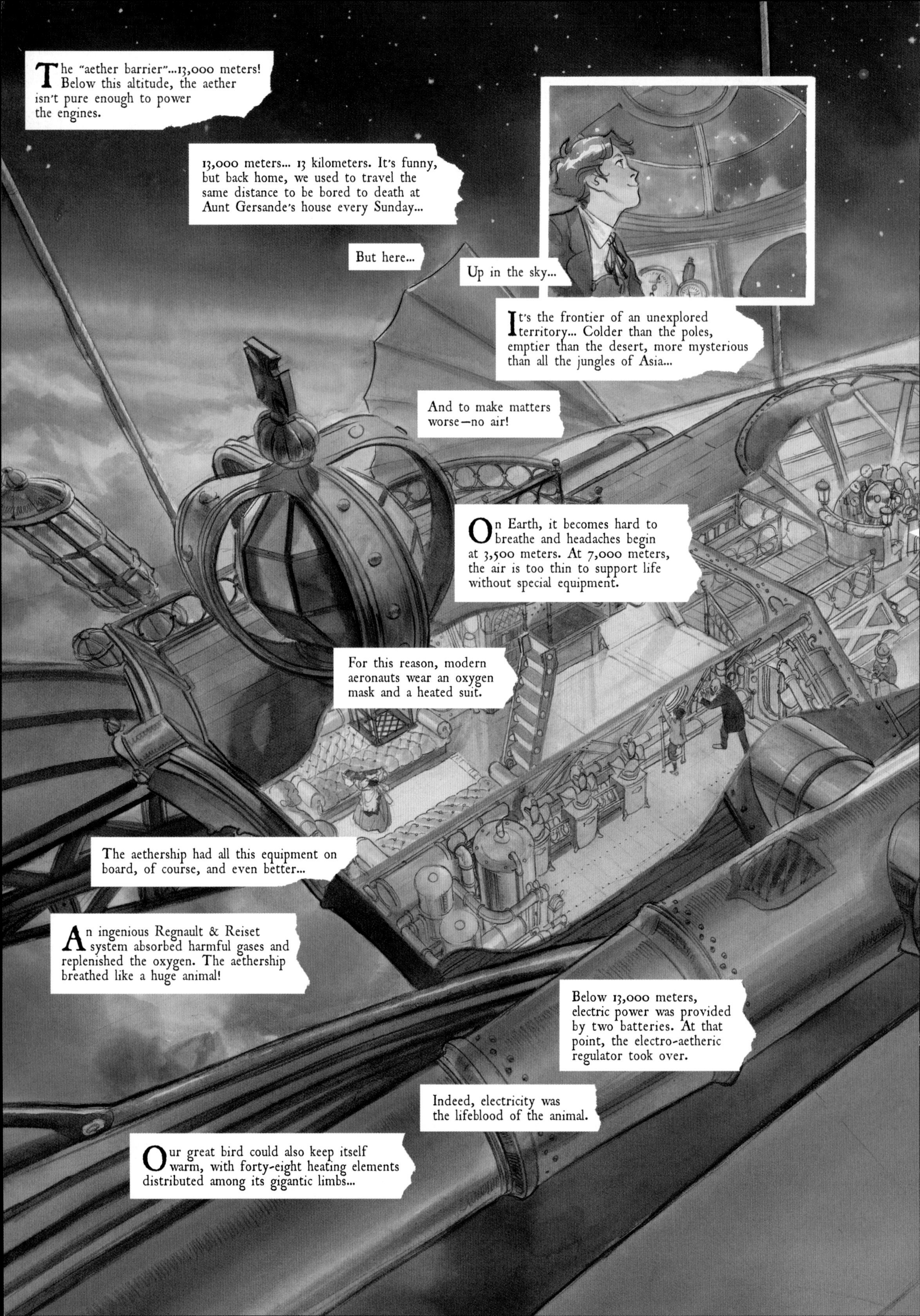
The "aether barrier"...13,000 meters! Below this altitude, the aether isn't pure enough to power the engines.
13,000 meters... 13 kilometers. It's funny, but back home, we used to travel the same distance to be bored to death at Aunt Gersande's house every Sunday...
But here...
Up in the sky...
It's the frontier of an unexplored territory... Colder than the poles, emptier than the desert, more mysterious than all the jungles of Asia...
And to make matters worse—no air!
On Earth, it becomes hard to breathe and headaches begin at 3,500 meters. At 7,000 meters, the air is too thin to support life without special equipment.
For this reason, modern aeronauts wear an oxygen mask and a heated suit.
The aethership had all this equipment on board, of course, and even better...
An ingenious Regnault & Reiset system absorbed harmful gases and replenished the oxygen. The aethership breathed like a huge animal!
Below 13,000 meters, electric power was provided by two batteries. At that point, the electro-aetheric regulator took over.
Indeed, electricity was the lifeblood of the animal.
Our great bird could also keep itself warm, with forty-eight heating elements distributed among its gigantic limbs...

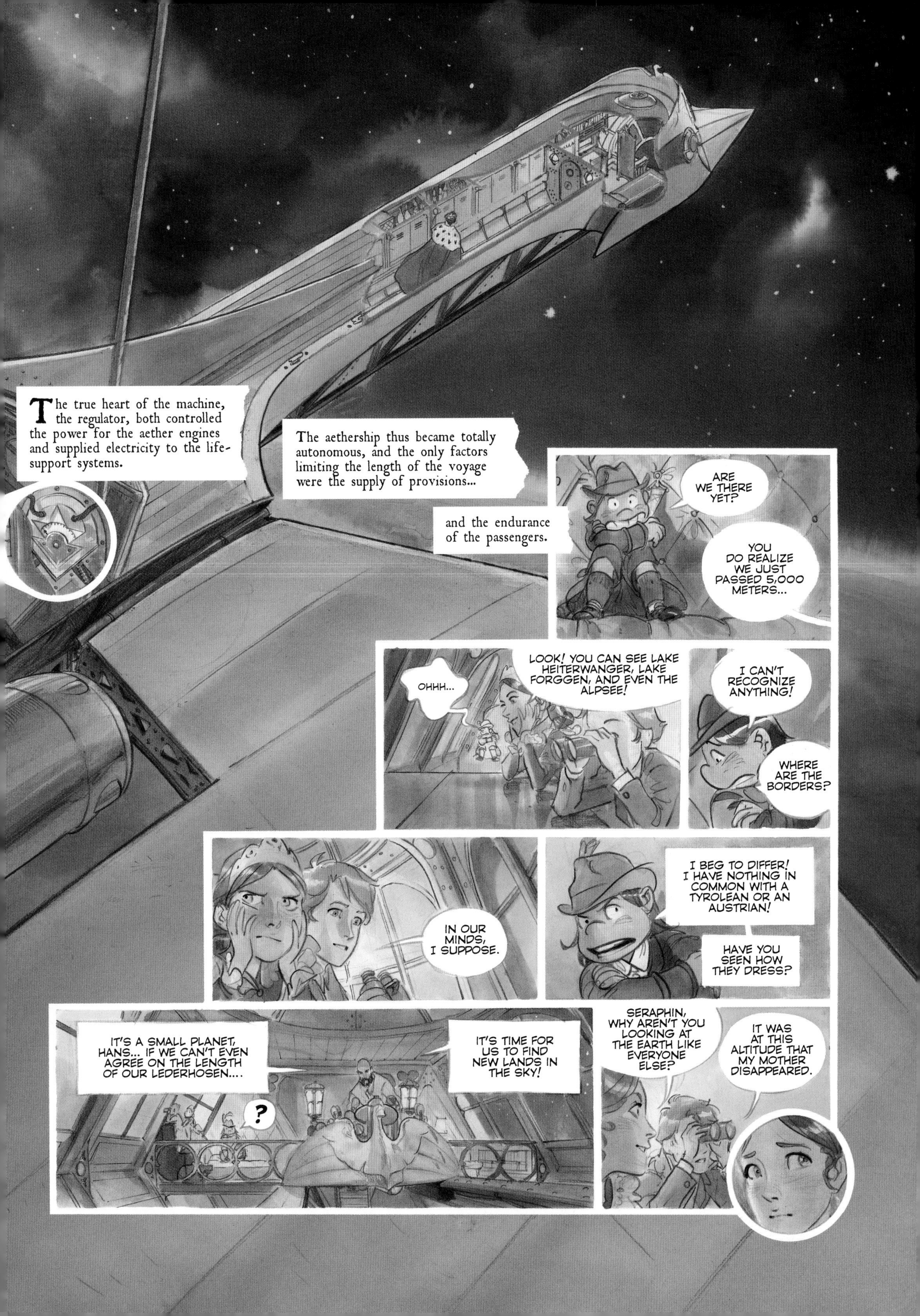
The true heart of the machine, the regulator, both controlled the power for the aether engines and supplied electricity to the life-support systems.
The aethership thus became totally autonomous, and the only factors limiting the length of the voyage were the supply of provisions...
and the endurance of the passengers.
ARE WE THERE YET?
YOU DO REALIZE WE JUST PASSED 5,000 METERS...
OHHH...
LOOK! YOU CAN SEE LAKE HEITERWANGER, LAKE FORGGEN, AND EVEN THE ALPSEE!
I CAN'T RECOGNIZE ANYTHING!
WHERE ARE THE BORDERS?
IN OUR MINDS, I SUPPOSE.
I BEG TO DIFFER! I HAVE NOTHING IN COMMON WITH A TYROLEAN OR AN AUSTRIAN!
HAVE YOU SEEN HOW THEY DRESS?
IT'S A SMALL PLANET, HANS... IF WE CAN'T EVEN AGREE ON THE LENGTH OF OUR LEDERHOSEN....
?
IT'S TIME FOR US TO FIND NEW LANDS IN THE SKY!
SERAPHIN, WHY AREN'T YOU LOOKING AT THE EARTH LIKE EVERYONE ELSE?
IT WAS AT THIS ALTITUDE THAT MY MOTHER DISAPPEARED.

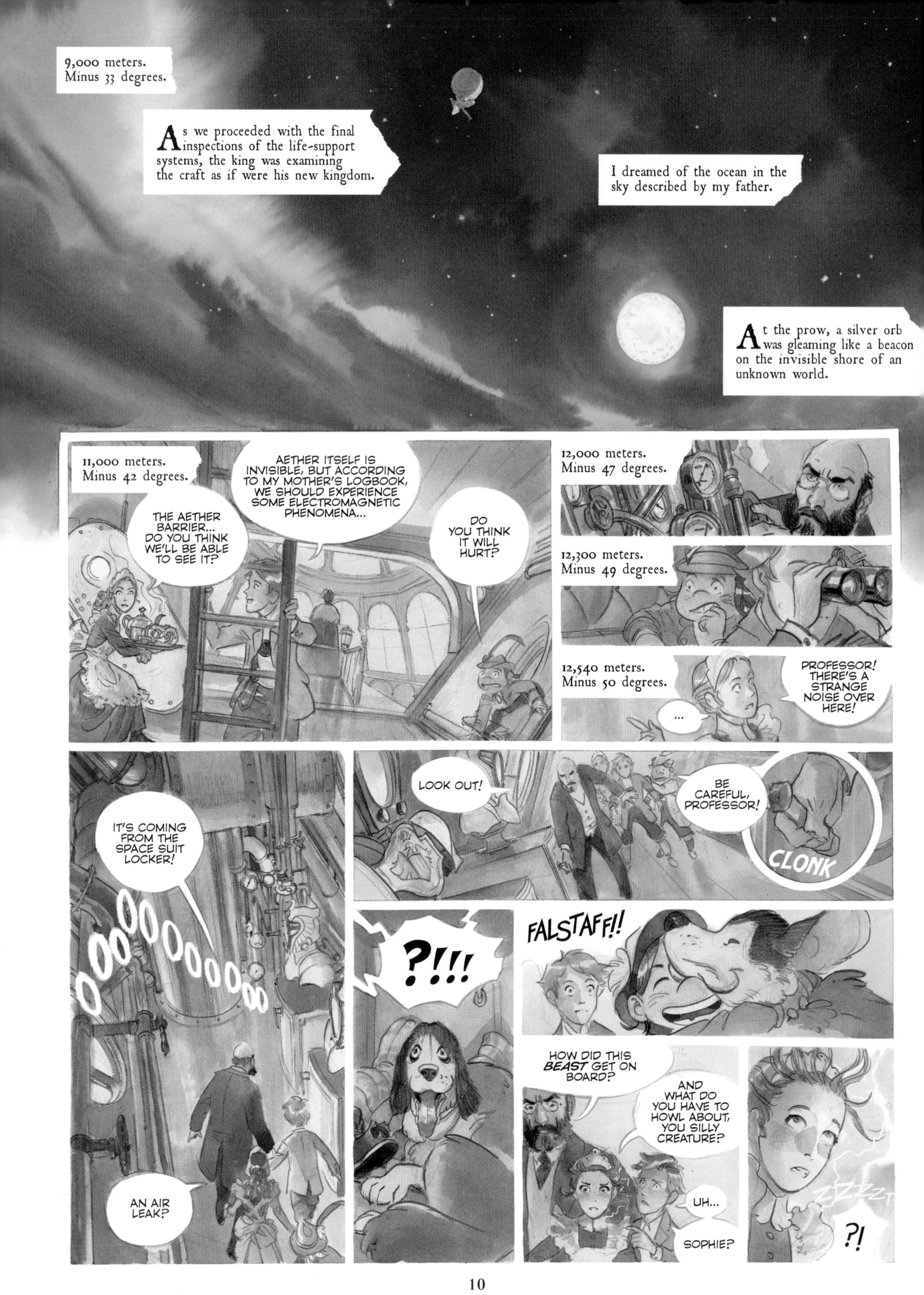
9,000 meters.
Minus 33 degrees.
As we proceeded with the final inspections of the life-support systems, the king was examining the craft as if were his new kingdom.
I dreamed of the ocean in the sky described by my father.
At the prow, a silver orb was gleaming like a beacon on the invisible shore of an unknown world.
11,000 meters.
Minus 42 degrees.
THE AETHER BARRIER... DO YOU THINK WE'LL BE ABLE TO SEE IT?
AETHER ITSELF IS INVISIBLE, BUT ACCORDING TO MY MOTHER'S LOGBOOK, WE SHOULD EXPERIENCE SOME ELECTROMAGNETIC PHENOMENA...
DO YOU THINK IT WILL HURT?
12,000 meters.
Minus 47 degrees.
12,300 meters.
Minus 49 degrees.
12,540 meters.
Minus 50 degrees.
...
PROFESSOR! THERE'S A STRANGE NOISE OVER HERE!
IT'S COMING FROM THE SPACE SUIT LOCKER!
OOOOOOOOOOOO
AN AIR LEAK?
LOOK OUT!
BE CAREFUL, PROFESSOR!
CLONK
?!!!
FALSTAFF!!
HOW DID THIS BEAST GET ON BOARD?
AND WHAT DO YOU HAVE TO HOWL ABOUT, YOU SILLY CREATURE?
UH...
SOPHIE?
ZZZZT
?!

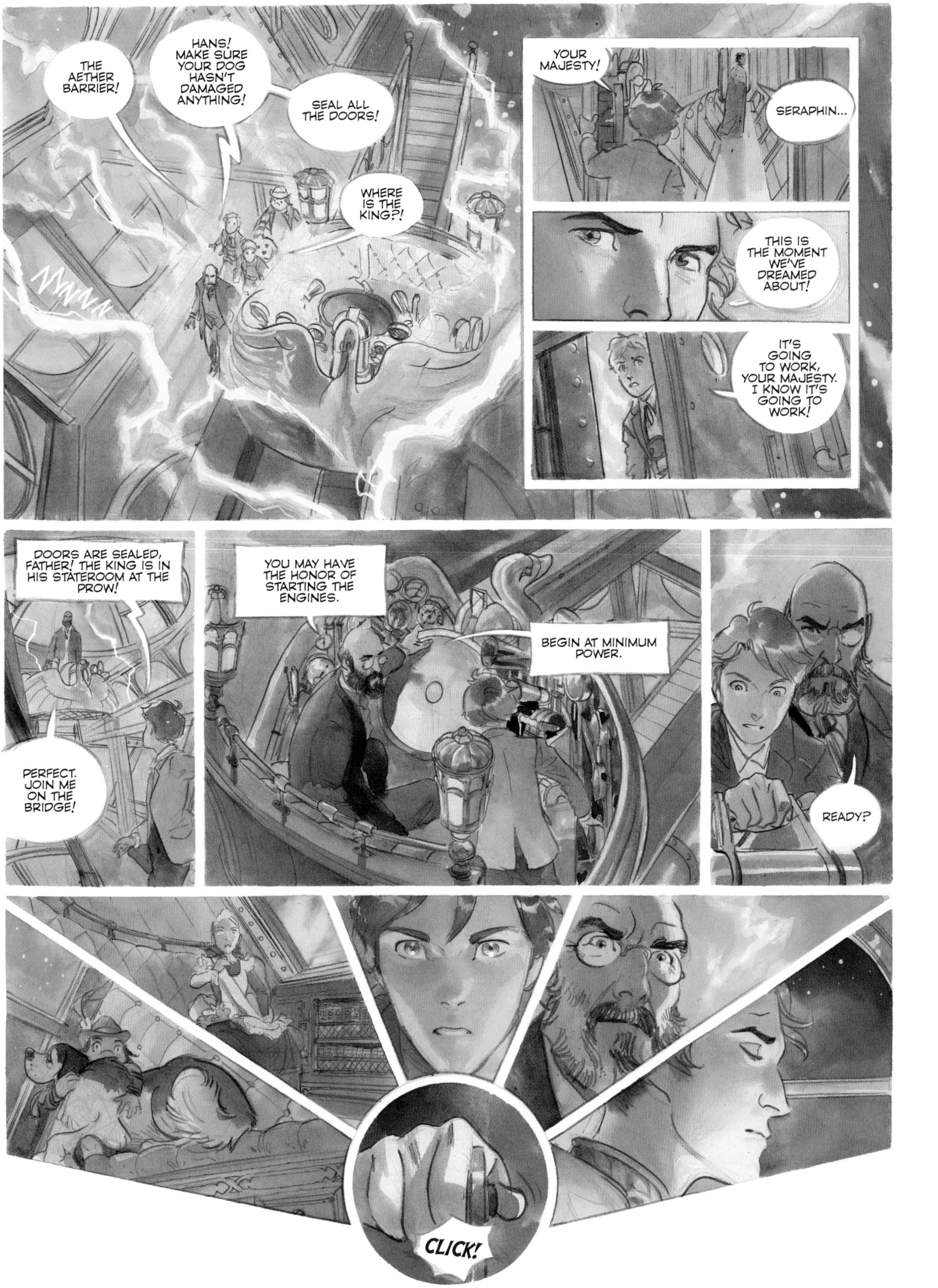
THE AETHER BARRIER!
HANS! MAKE SURE YOUR DOG HASN'T DAMAGED ANYTHING!
SEAL ALL THE DOORS!
WHERE IS THE KING?!
YOUR MAJESTY!
SERAPHIN...
THIS IS THE MOMENT WE'VE DREAMED ABOUT!
IT'S GOING TO WORK, YOUR MAJESTY. I KNOW IT'S GOING TO WORK!
DOORS ARE SEALED, FATHER! THE KING IS IN HIS STATEROOM AT THE PROW!
PERFECT. JOIN ME ON THE BRIDGE!
YOU MAY HAVE THE HONOR OF STARTING THE ENGINES.
BEGIN AT MINIMUM POWER.
READY?
CLICK!

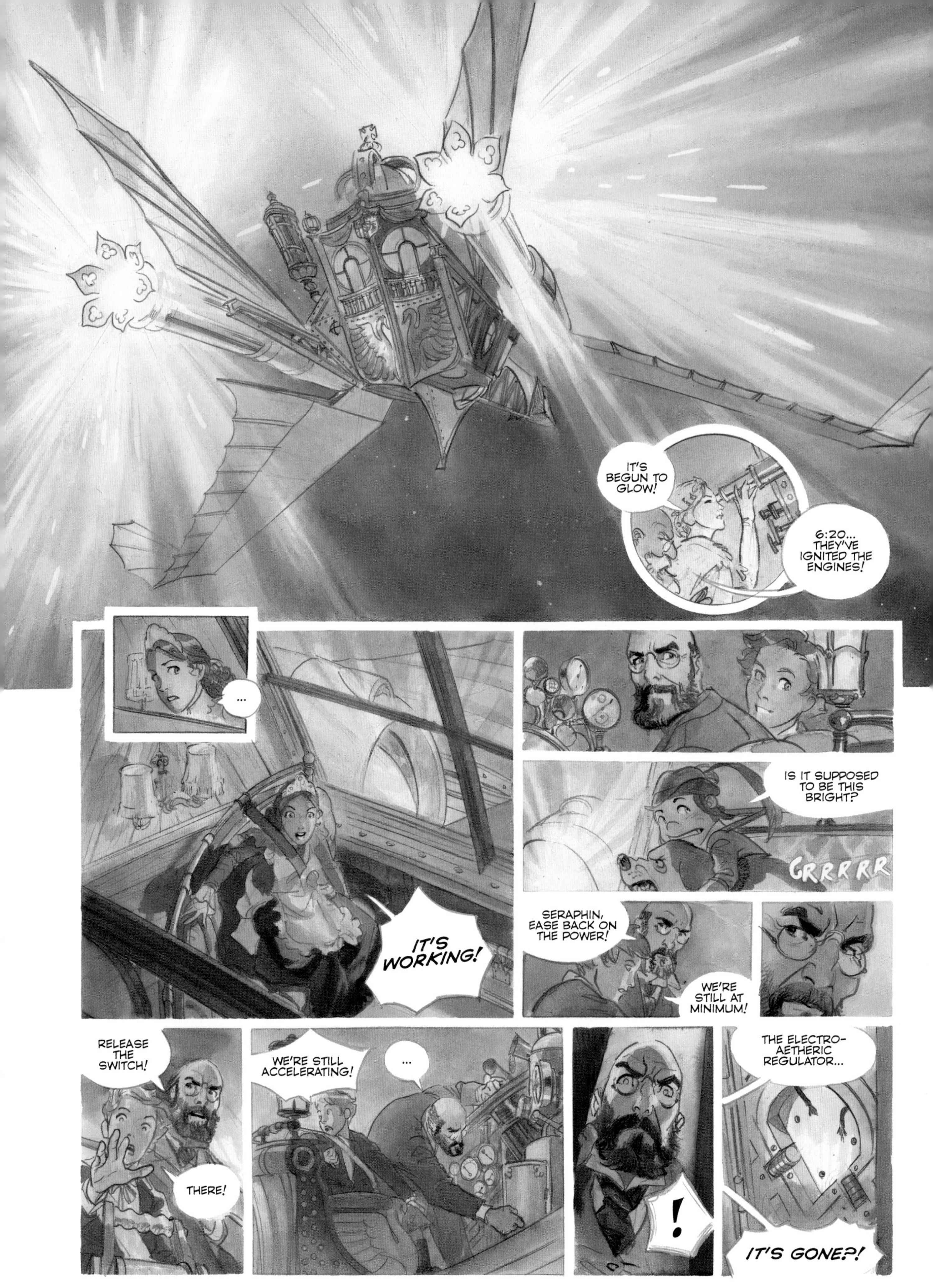
IT'S BEGUN TO GLOW!
6:20... THEY'VE IGNITED THE ENGINES!
...
IT'S WORKING!
IS IT SUPPOSED TO BE THIS BRIGHT?
GRRRRR
SERAPHIN, EASE BACK ON THE POWER!
WE'RE STILL AT MINIMUM!
RELEASE THE SWITCH!
THERE!
WE'RE STILL ACCELERATING!
...
!
THE ELECTRO-AETHERIC REGULATOR...
IT'S GONE?!

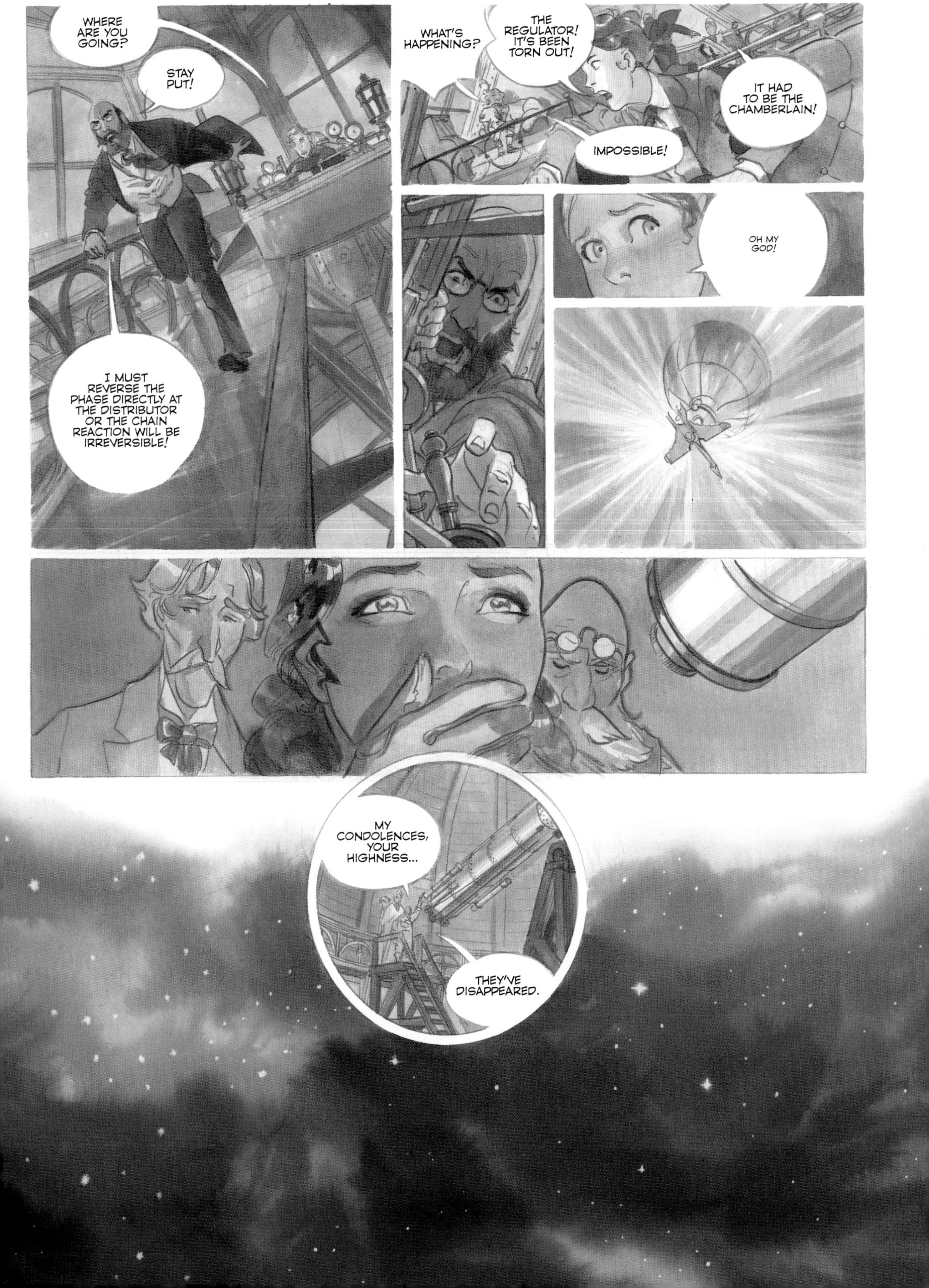

WHERE ARE YOU GOING?
STAY PUT!
I MUST REVERSE THE PHASE DIRECTLY AT THE DISTRIBUTOR OR THE CHAIN REACTION WILL BE IRREVERSIBLE!
WHAT'S HAPPENING?
THE REGULATOR! IT'S BEEN TORN OUT!
IT HAD TO BE THE CHAMBERLAIN!
IMPOSSIBLE!
OH MY GOD!
MY CONDOLENCES, YOUR HIGHNESS...
THEY'VE DISAPPEARED.

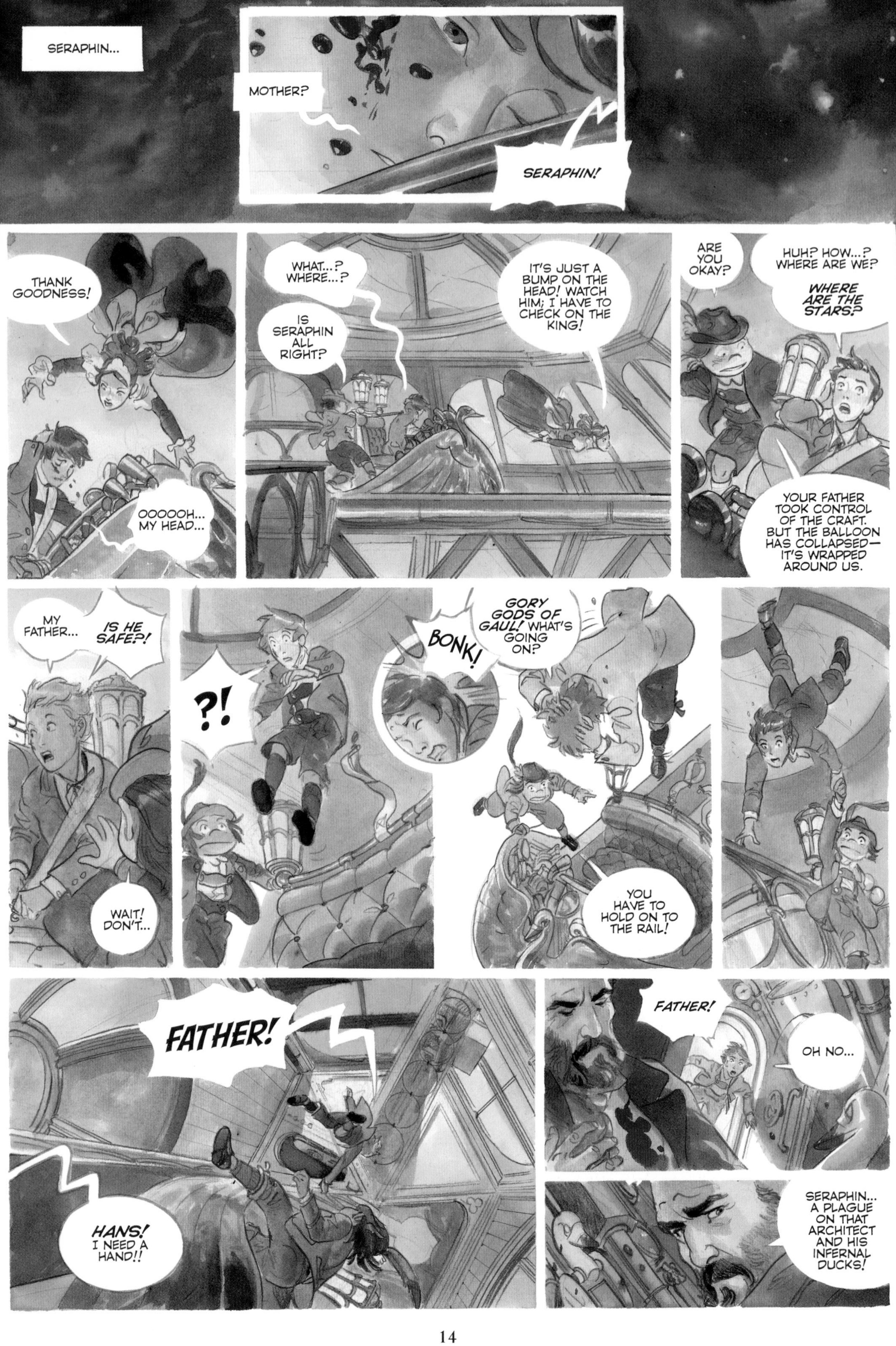

SERAPHIN...
MOTHER?
SERAPHIN!
THANK GOODNESS!
OOOOOH... MY HEAD...
WHAT...? WHERE...?
IS SERAPHIN ALL RIGHT?
IT'S JUST A BUMP ON THE HEAD! WATCH HIM; I HAVE TO CHECK ON THE KING!
ARE YOU OKAY?
HUH? HOW...? WHERE ARE WE? WHERE ARE THE STARS?
YOUR FATHER TOOK CONTROL OF THE CRAFT. BUT THE BALLOON HAS COLLAPSED—IT'S WRAPPED AROUND US.
MY FATHER... IS HE SAFE?!
WAIT! DON'T...
?!
BONK!
GORY GODS OF GAUL! WHAT'S GOING ON?
YOU HAVE TO HOLD ON TO THE RAIL!
FATHER!
HANS! I NEED A HAND!!
FATHER!
OH NO...
SERAPHIN... A PLAGUE ON THAT ARCHITECT AND HIS INFERNAL DUCKS!

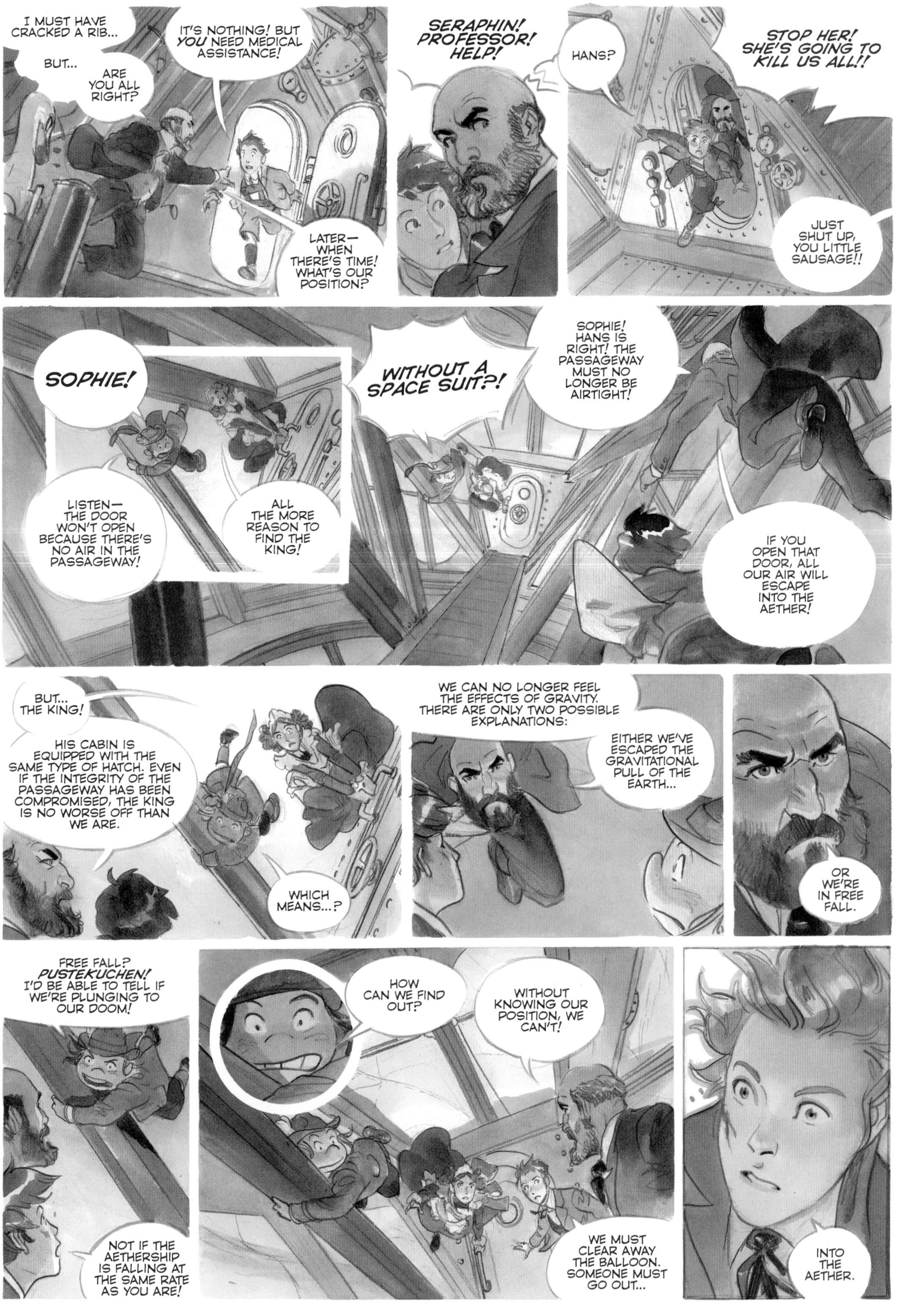

I MUST HAVE CRACKED A RIB...
BUT... ARE YOU ALL RIGHT?
IT'S NOTHING! BUT *YOU* NEED MEDICAL ASSISTANCE!
LATER— WHEN THERE'S TIME! WHAT'S OUR POSITION?
SERAPHIN! PROFESSOR! HELP!
HANS?
STOP HER! SHE'S GOING TO KILL US ALL!!
JUST SHUT UP, YOU LITTLE SAUSAGE!!
SOPHIE!
LISTEN— THE DOOR WON'T OPEN BECAUSE THERE'S NO AIR IN THE PASSAGEWAY!
ALL THE MORE REASON TO FIND THE KING!
WITHOUT A SPACE SUIT?!
SOPHIE! HANS IS RIGHT! THE PASSAGEWAY MUST NO LONGER BE AIRTIGHT!
IF YOU OPEN THAT DOOR, ALL OUR AIR WILL ESCAPE INTO THE AETHER!
BUT... THE KING!
HIS CABIN IS EQUIPPED WITH THE SAME TYPE OF HATCH. EVEN IF THE INTEGRITY OF THE PASSAGEWAY HAS BEEN COMPROMISED, THE KING IS NO WORSE OFF THAN WE ARE.
WHICH MEANS...?
WE CAN NO LONGER FEEL THE EFFECTS OF GRAVITY. THERE ARE ONLY TWO POSSIBLE EXPLANATIONS:
EITHER WE'VE ESCAPED THE GRAVITATIONAL PULL OF THE EARTH...
OR WE'RE IN FREE FALL.
FREE FALL? *PUSTEKUCHEN!* I'D BE ABLE TO TELL IF WE'RE PLUNGING TO OUR DOOM!
NOT IF THE AETHERSHIP IS FALLING AT THE SAME RATE AS YOU ARE!
HOW CAN WE FIND OUT?
WITHOUT KNOWING OUR POSITION, WE CAN'T!
WE MUST CLEAR AWAY THE BALLOON. SOMEONE MUST GO OUT...
INTO THE AETHER.

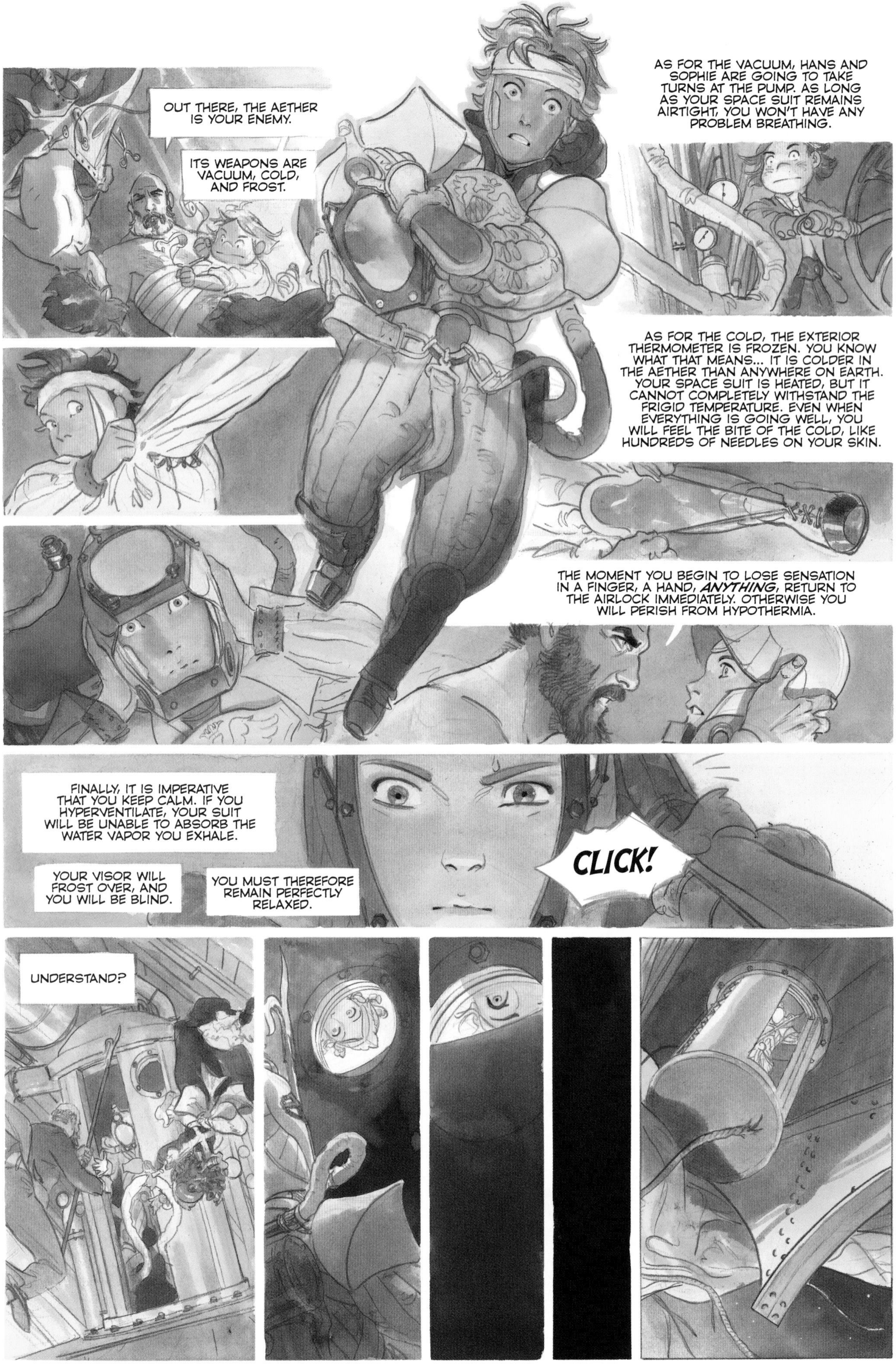
OUT THERE, THE AETHER IS YOUR ENEMY.
ITS WEAPONS ARE VACUUM, COLD, AND FROST.
AS FOR THE VACUUM, HANS AND SOPHIE ARE GOING TO TAKE TURNS AT THE PUMP. AS LONG AS YOUR SPACE SUIT REMAINS AIRTIGHT, YOU WON'T HAVE ANY PROBLEM BREATHING.
AS FOR THE COLD, THE EXTERIOR THERMOMETER IS FROZEN. YOU KNOW WHAT THAT MEANS... IT IS COLDER IN THE AETHER THAN ANYWHERE ON EARTH. YOUR SPACE SUIT IS HEATED, BUT IT CANNOT COMPLETELY WITHSTAND THE FRIGID TEMPERATURE. EVEN WHEN EVERYTHING IS GOING WELL, YOU WILL FEEL THE BITE OF THE COLD, LIKE HUNDREDS OF NEEDLES ON YOUR SKIN.
THE MOMENT YOU BEGIN TO LOSE SENSATION IN A FINGER, A HAND, *ANYTHING*, RETURN TO THE AIRLOCK IMMEDIATELY. OTHERWISE YOU WILL PERISH FROM HYPOTHERMIA.
FINALLY, IT IS IMPERATIVE THAT YOU KEEP CALM. IF YOU HYPERVENTILATE, YOUR SUIT WILL BE UNABLE TO ABSORB THE WATER VAPOR YOU EXHALE.
YOUR VISOR WILL FROST OVER, AND YOU WILL BE BLIND.
YOU MUST THEREFORE REMAIN PERFECTLY RELAXED.
CLICK!
UNDERSTAND?

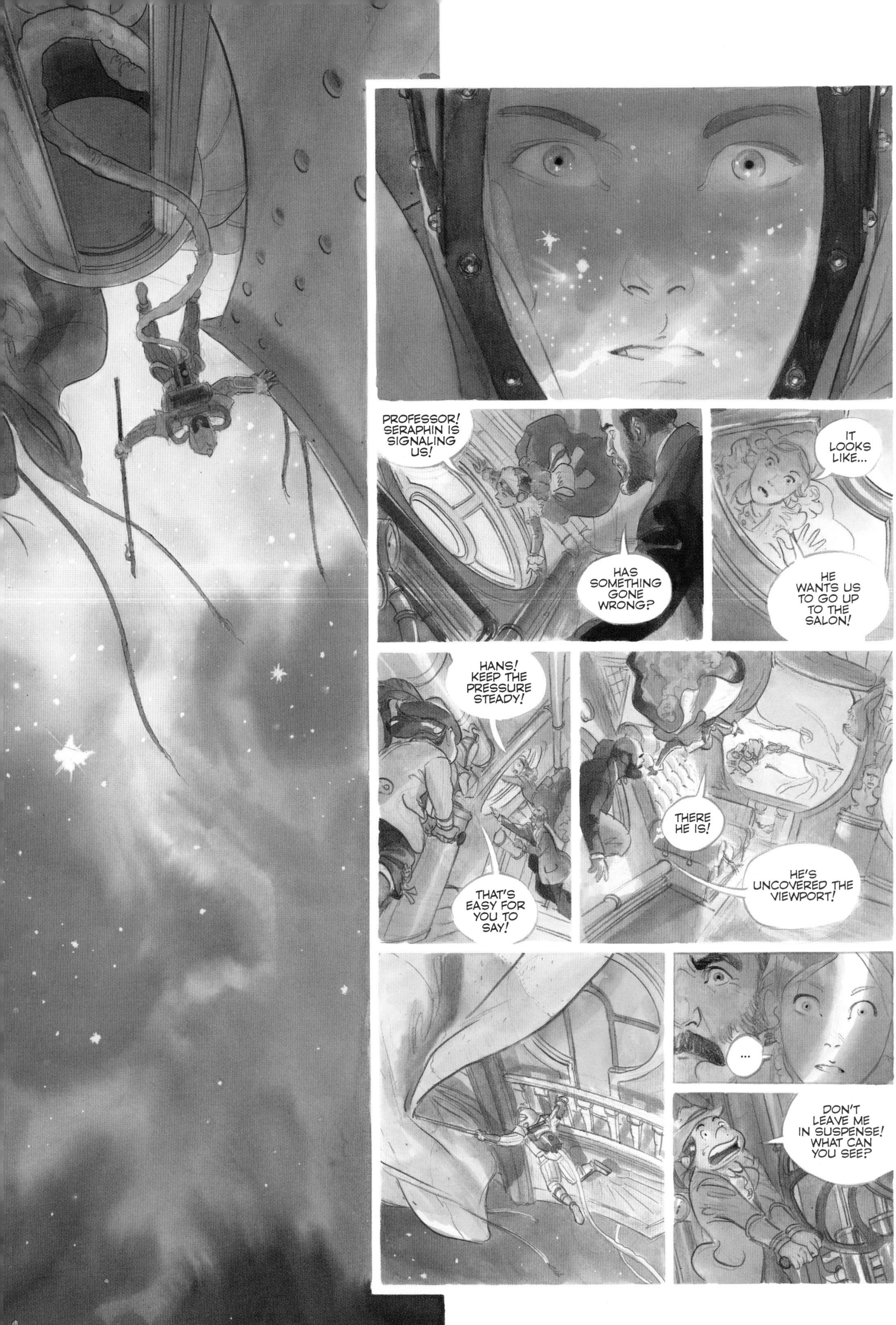
PROFESSOR! SERAPHIN IS SIGNALING US!
HAS SOMETHING GONE WRONG?
IT LOOKS LIKE...
HE WANTS US TO GO UP TO THE SALON!
HANS! KEEP THE PRESSURE STEADY!
THAT'S EASY FOR YOU TO SAY!
THERE HE IS!
HE'S UNCOVERED THE VIEWPORT!
...
DON'T LEAVE ME IN SUSPENSE! WHAT CAN YOU SEE?

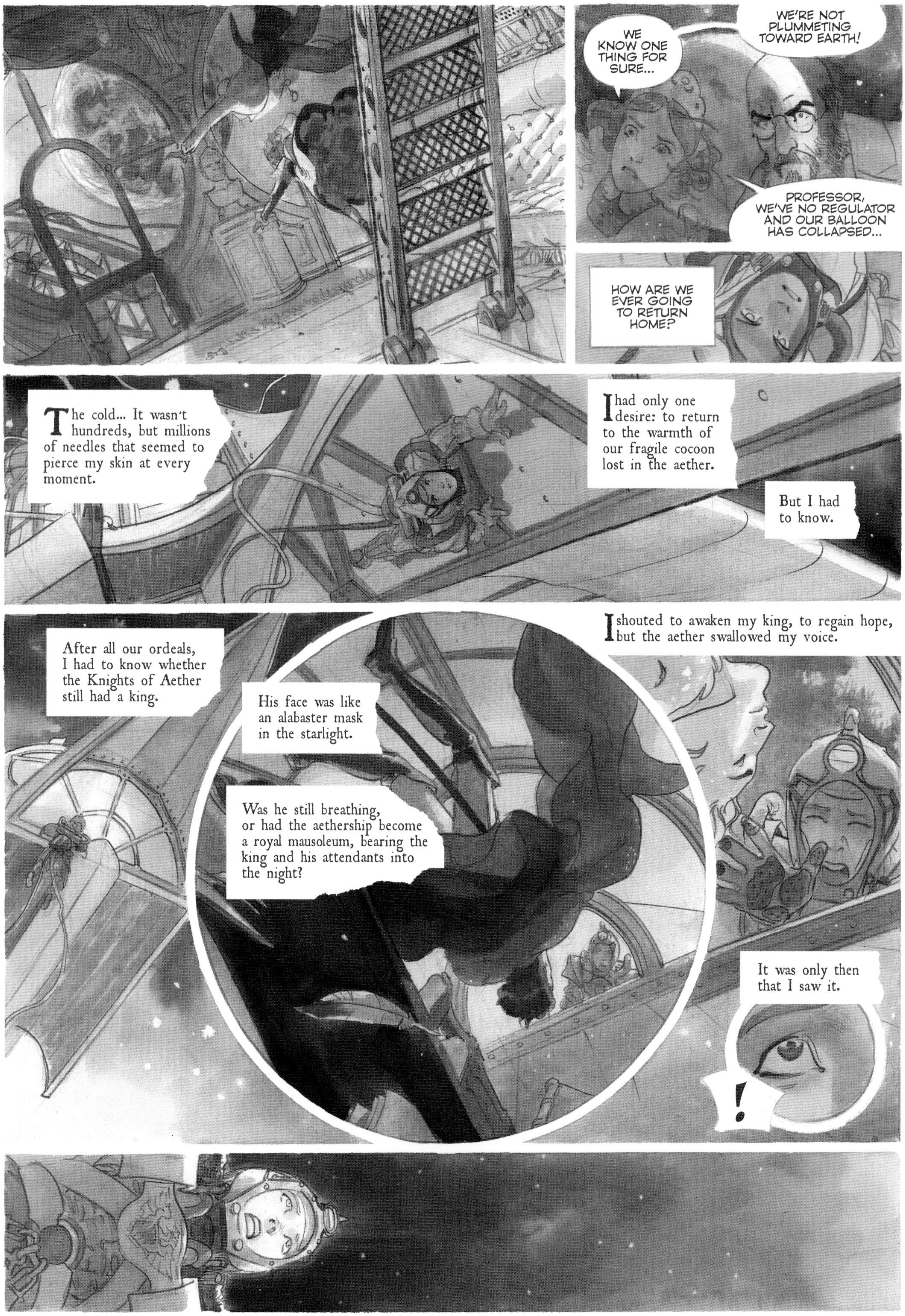
WE KNOW ONE THING FOR SURE...
WE'RE NOT PLUMMETING TOWARD EARTH!
PROFESSOR, WE'VE NO REGULATOR AND OUR BALLOON HAS COLLAPSED...
HOW ARE WE EVER GOING TO RETURN HOME?
The cold... It wasn't hundreds, but millions of needles that seemed to pierce my skin at every moment.
I had only one desire: to return to the warmth of our fragile cocoon lost in the aether.
But I had to know.
After all our ordeals, I had to know whether the Knights of Aether still had a king.
His face was like an alabaster mask in the starlight.
Was he still breathing, or had the aethership become a royal mausoleum, bearing the king and his attendants into the night?
I shouted to awaken my king, to regain hope, but the aether swallowed my voice.
It was only then that I saw it.
!

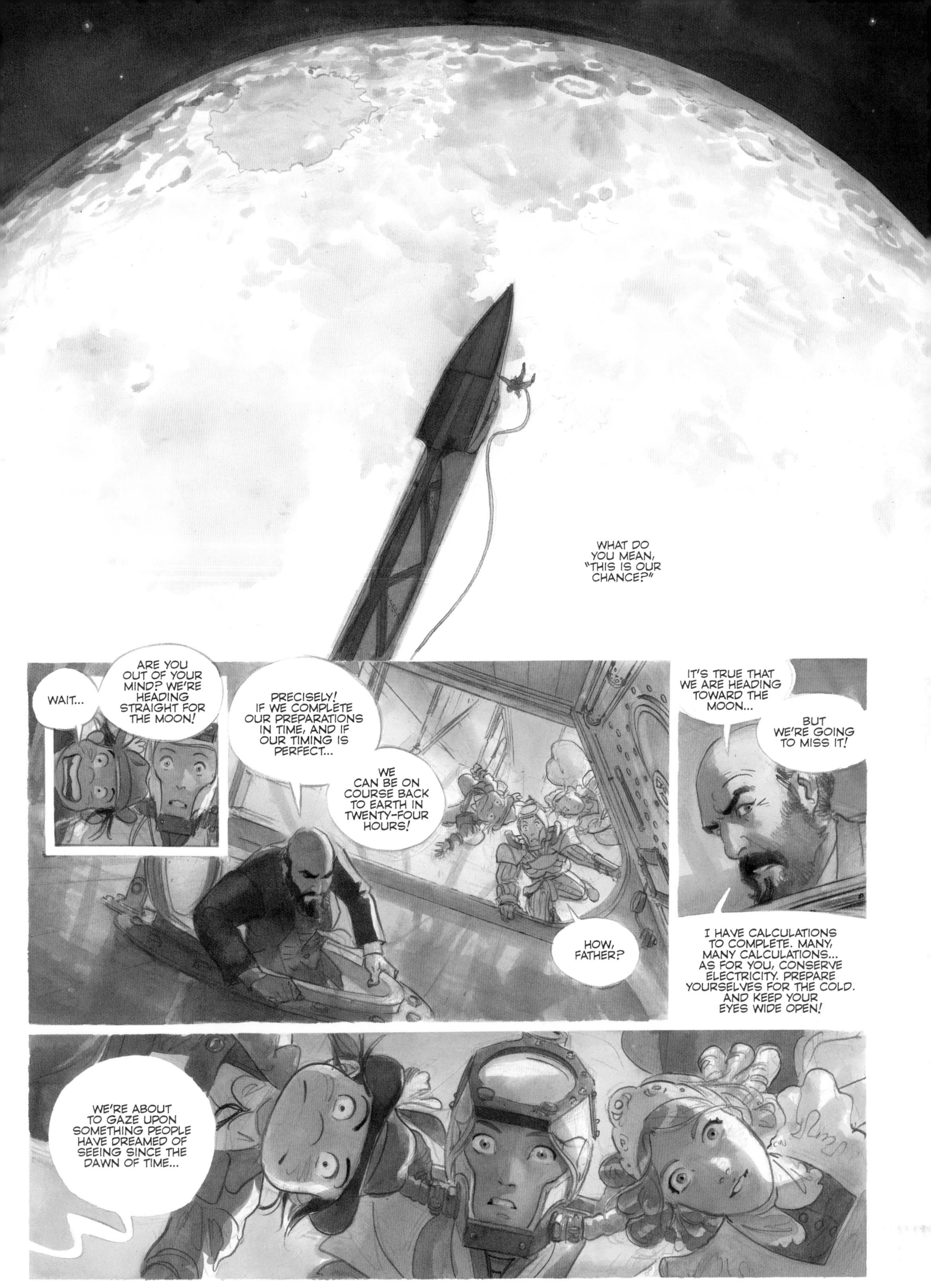
WHAT DO YOU MEAN, "THIS IS OUR CHANCE?"
WAIT...
ARE YOU OUT OF YOUR MIND? WE'RE HEADING STRAIGHT FOR THE MOON!
PRECISELY! IF WE COMPLETE OUR PREPARATIONS IN TIME, AND IF OUR TIMING IS PERFECT...
WE CAN BE ON COURSE BACK TO EARTH IN TWENTY-FOUR HOURS!
HOW, FATHER?
IT'S TRUE THAT WE ARE HEADING TOWARD THE MOON...
BUT WE'RE GOING TO MISS IT!
I HAVE CALCULATIONS TO COMPLETE. MANY, MANY CALCULATIONS... AS FOR YOU, CONSERVE ELECTRICITY. PREPARE YOURSELVES FOR THE COLD. AND KEEP YOUR EYES WIDE OPEN!
WE'RE ABOUT TO GAZE UPON SOMETHING PEOPLE HAVE DREAMED OF SEEING SINCE THE DAWN OF TIME...

CHAPTER 5

SECRETS OF THE DARK SIDE

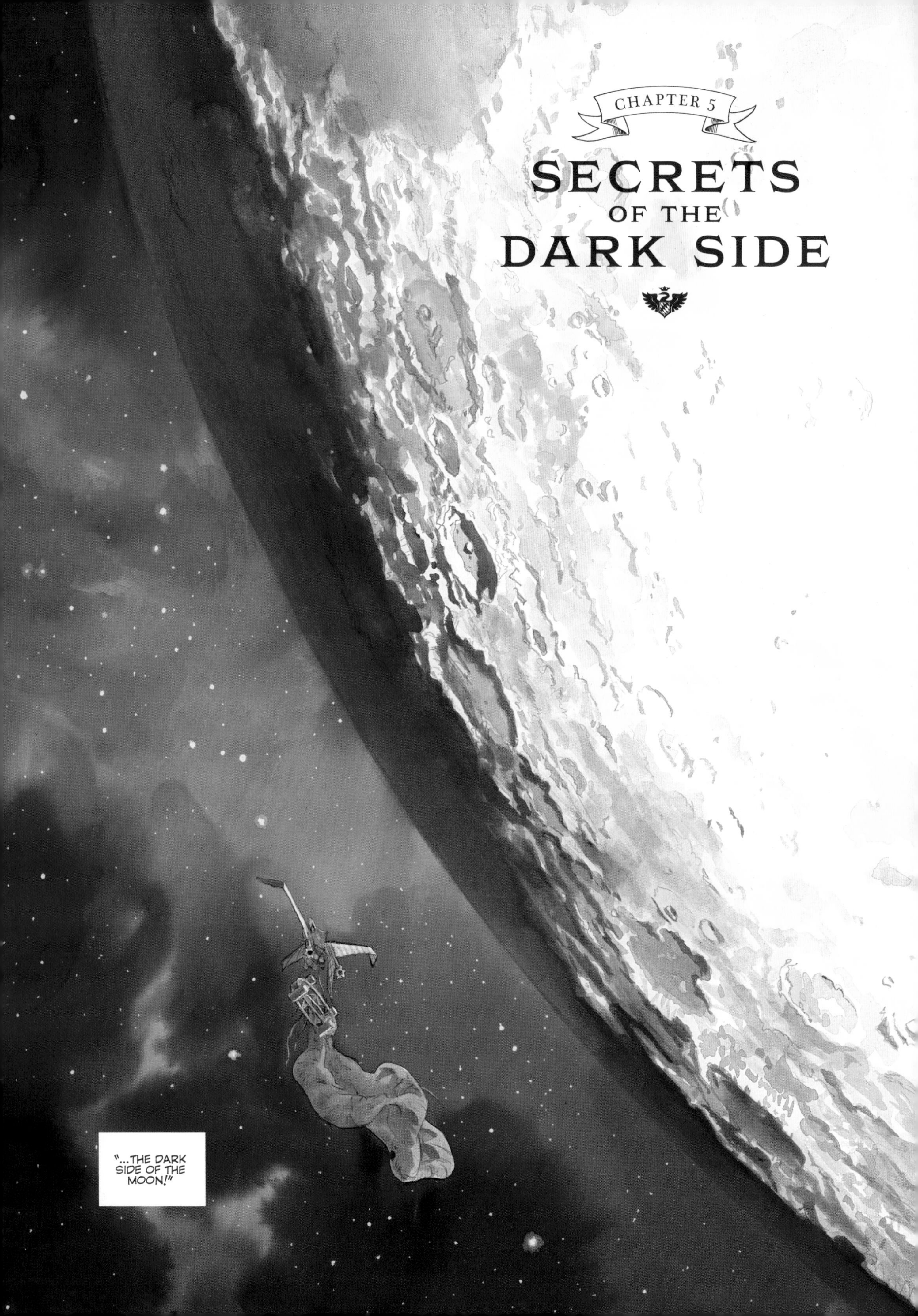
"...THE DARK SIDE OF THE MOON!"

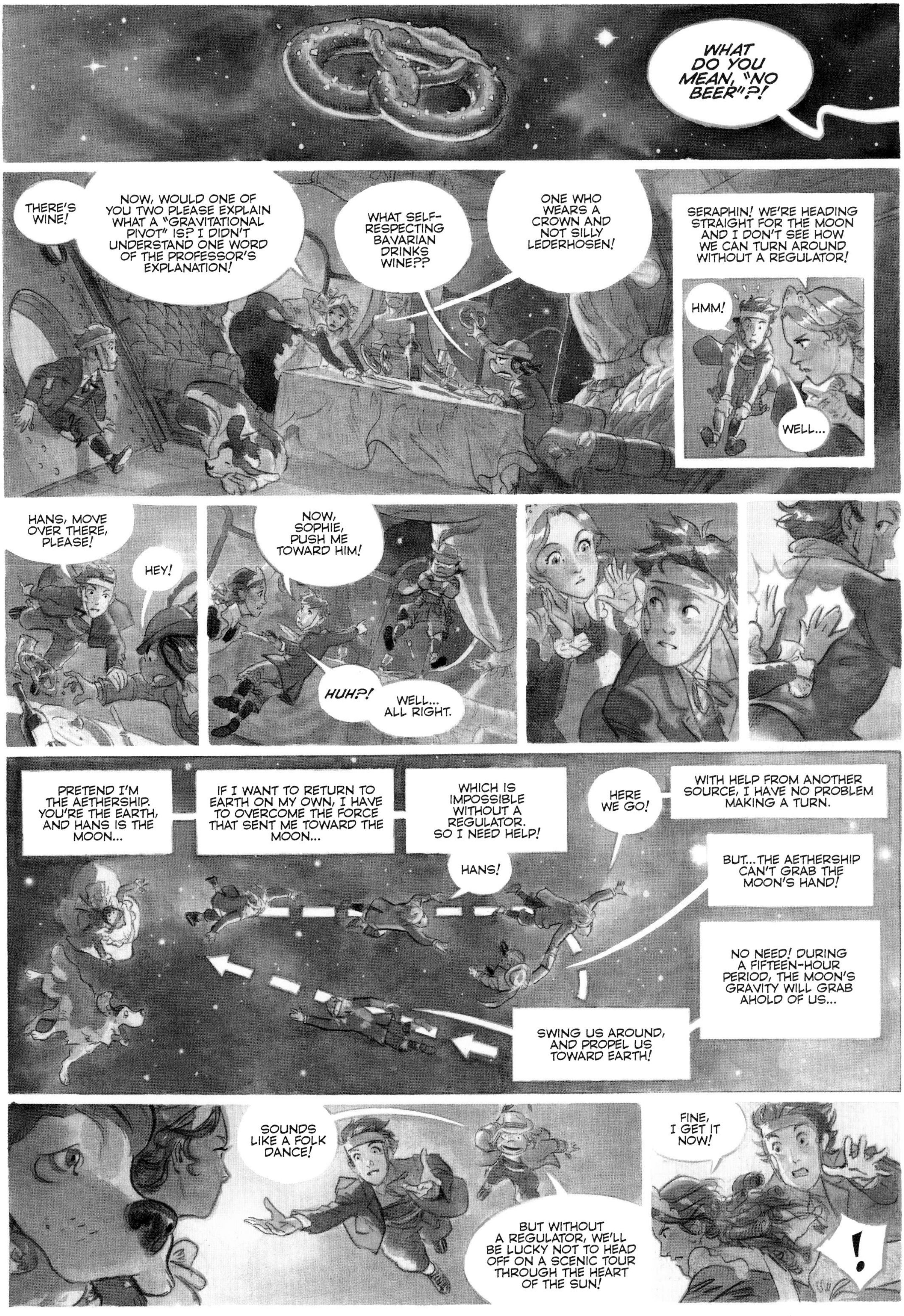
WHAT DO YOU MEAN, "NO BEER"?!
THERE'S WINE!
NOW, WOULD ONE OF YOU TWO PLEASE EXPLAIN WHAT A "GRAVITATIONAL PIVOT" IS? I DIDN'T UNDERSTAND ONE WORD OF THE PROFESSOR'S EXPLANATION!
WHAT SELF-RESPECTING BAVARIAN DRINKS WINE??
ONE WHO WEARS A CROWN AND NOT SILLY LEDERHOSEN!
SERAPHIN! WE'RE HEADING STRAIGHT FOR THE MOON AND I DON'T SEE HOW WE CAN TURN AROUND WITHOUT A REGULATOR!
HMM!
WELL...
HANS, MOVE OVER THERE, PLEASE!
HEY!
NOW, SOPHIE, PUSH ME TOWARD HIM!
HUH?!
WELL... ALL RIGHT.
PRETEND I'M THE AETHERSHIP. YOU'RE THE EARTH, AND HANS IS THE MOON...
IF I WANT TO RETURN TO EARTH ON MY OWN, I HAVE TO OVERCOME THE FORCE THAT SENT ME TOWARD THE MOON...
WHICH IS IMPOSSIBLE WITHOUT A REGULATOR. SO I NEED HELP!
HANS!
HERE WE GO!
WITH HELP FROM ANOTHER SOURCE, I HAVE NO PROBLEM MAKING A TURN.
BUT...THE AETHERSHIP CAN'T GRAB THE MOON'S HAND!
NO NEED! DURING A FIFTEEN-HOUR PERIOD, THE MOON'S GRAVITY WILL GRAB AHOLD OF US...
SWING US AROUND, AND PROPEL US TOWARD EARTH!
SOUNDS LIKE A FOLK DANCE!
BUT WITHOUT A REGULATOR, WE'LL BE LUCKY NOT TO HEAD OFF ON A SCENIC TOUR THROUGH THE HEART OF THE SUN!
FINE, I GET IT NOW!
!

SOPHIE! WHERE ARE YOU GOING?

FIFTEEN HOURS BEHIND THE MOON! WITHOUT THE SUN, WE'LL HAVE NO HEAT! NO WONDER YOUR FATHER ORDERED US TO PREPARE FOR THE COLD!

BUT...WHAT DO YOU HAVE IN MIND?!

I'M GOING TO FIND THE KING!

HUH?!

THERE'S A SPACE SUIT IN HIS SIZE, ISN'T THERE?

BUT, SOPHIE... THERE'S NO AIRLOCK UP THERE! YOU WON'T BE ABLE TO OPEN THE KING'S CABIN WITHOUT LOSING ALL THE AIR!

... AT LEAST I'LL BE ABLE TO WARN HIM!

NOW SHOO! CAN'T YOU SEE I'M GETTING CHANGED?

I TRIED, SOPHIE. HE'S UNCONSCIOUS.

MAYBE EVEN...

SOPHIE, WE HAVE TO TRUST THE AETHERSHIP. AS MY FATHER SAYS... IF THE LIFE-SUPPORT SYSTEMS ARE WORKING...

THE KING IS NO WORSE OFF THAN WE ARE.

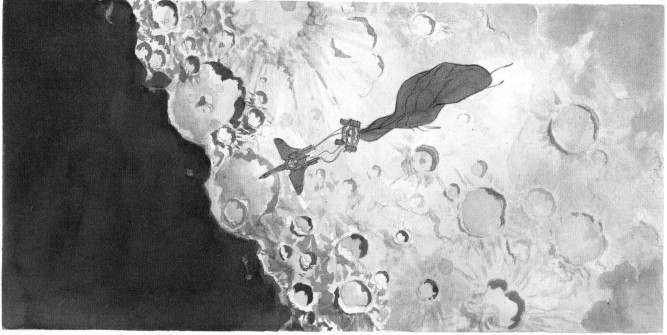

WE'RE PASSING OVER THE LUNAR TERMINATOR...

HAVE YOU EVER SEEN AN ECLIPSE?

THE WIND. THE SUDDEN COLD. THE DARKNESS.

WE DON'T REALIZE THE POWER OF THE SUN UNTIL IT'S GONE...

TAP TAP TAP TA

THAT SOUND...

DO YOU HEAR IT?

TAP TAP TAP TAP TAP TAP TAP

HANS! STOP THAT!

AREN'T YOU NERVOUS? WELL, *I'M* NERVOUS. AND WHEN I'M NERVOUS, I SMOKE!

ARE YOU KIDDING?! SMOKING WASTES FAR TOO MUCH OXYGEN.

YOU'RE NOT THE BOSS OF ME!

HANS...

PUT AWAY YOUR PIPE, PLEASE!

LOOK! THE EARTH!

IT'S DISAPPEARING!

FOR THE NEXT FIFTEEN HOURS, THE REST OF HUMANITY—EVERYTHING PEOPLE HAVE BUILT OR ACCOMPLISHED...

WILL BE HIDDEN FROM OUR EYES.

AND NOW, THE SUN...

AAOOOOOOOOOOOOOOO

SEE...

WE ARE THE ARCHITECTS OF OUR OWN ECLIPSE!

NOW OUR JOURNEY INTO THE UNKNOWN TRULY BEGINS.

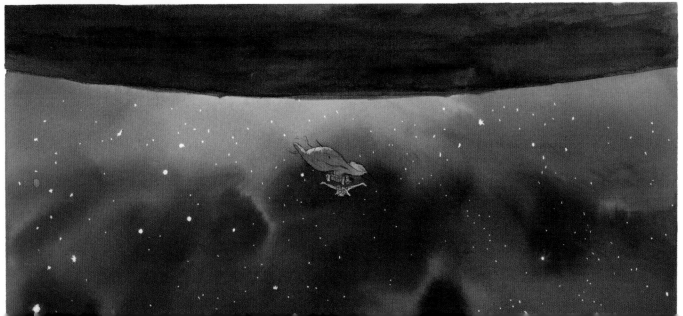

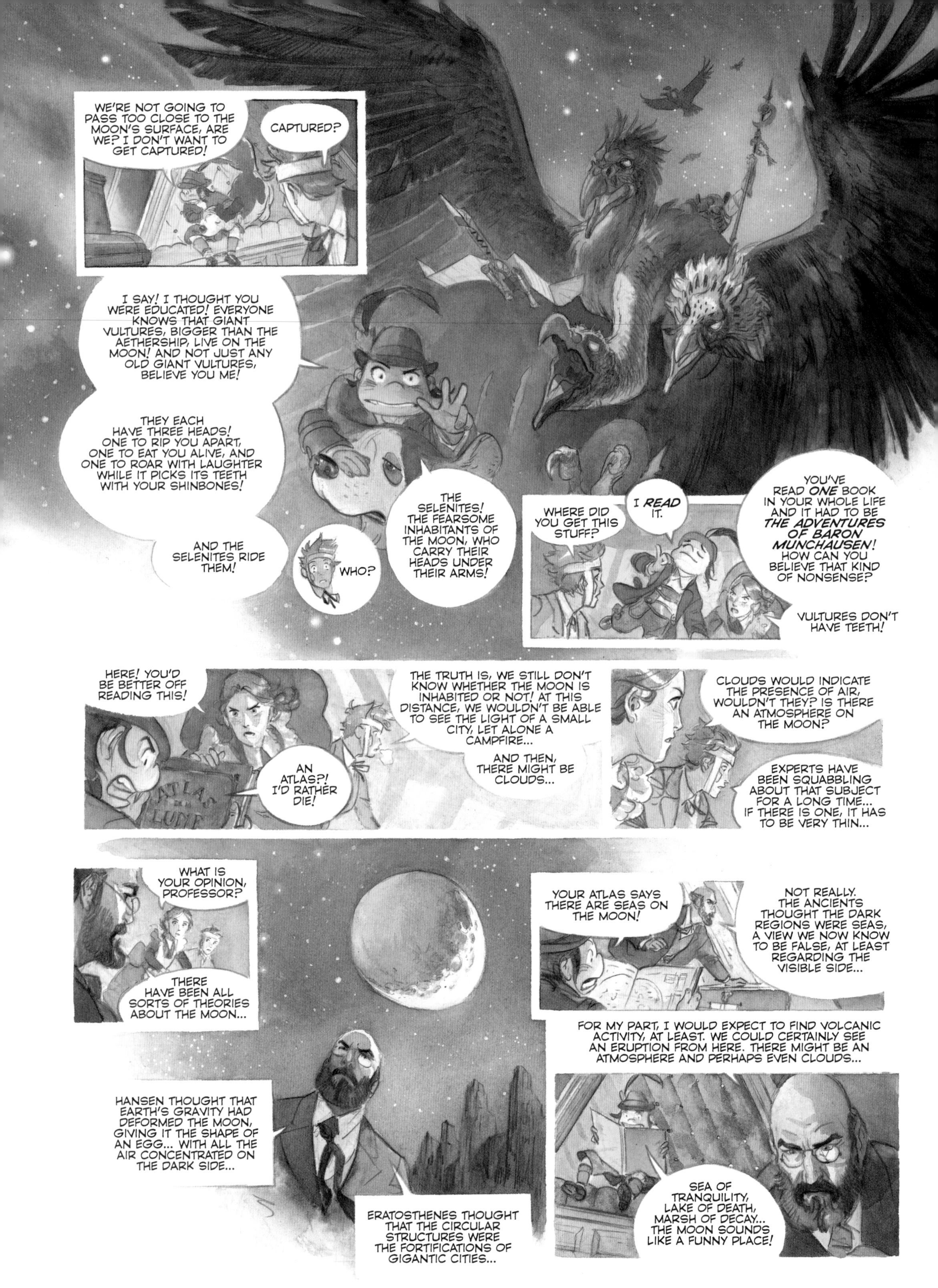

WE'RE NOT GOING TO PASS TOO CLOSE TO THE MOON'S SURFACE, ARE WE? I DON'T WANT TO GET CAPTURED!
CAPTURED?
I SAY! I THOUGHT YOU WERE EDUCATED! EVERYONE KNOWS THAT GIANT VULTURES, BIGGER THAN THE AETHERSHIP, LIVE ON THE MOON! AND NOT JUST ANY OLD GIANT VULTURES, BELIEVE YOU ME!
THEY EACH HAVE THREE HEADS! ONE TO RIP YOU APART, ONE TO EAT YOU ALIVE, AND ONE TO ROAR WITH LAUGHTER WHILE IT PICKS ITS TEETH WITH YOUR SHINBONES!
AND THE SELENITES RIDE THEM!
WHO?
THE SELENITES! THE FEARSOME INHABITANTS OF THE MOON, WHO CARRY THEIR HEADS UNDER THEIR ARMS!
WHERE DID YOU GET THIS STUFF?
I READ IT.
YOU'VE READ ONE BOOK IN YOUR WHOLE LIFE AND IT HAD TO BE THE ADVENTURES OF BARON MUNCHAUSEN! HOW CAN YOU BELIEVE THAT KIND OF NONSENSE?
VULTURES DON'T HAVE TEETH!
HERE! YOU'D BE BETTER OFF READING THIS!
AN ATLAS?! I'D RATHER DIE!
ATLAS DE LUNE
THE TRUTH IS, WE STILL DON'T KNOW WHETHER THE MOON IS INHABITED OR NOT! AT THIS DISTANCE, WE WOULDN'T BE ABLE TO SEE THE LIGHT OF A SMALL CITY, LET ALONE A CAMPFIRE...
AND THEN, THERE MIGHT BE CLOUDS...
CLOUDS WOULD INDICATE THE PRESENCE OF AIR, WOULDN'T THEY? IS THERE AN ATMOSPHERE ON THE MOON?
EXPERTS HAVE BEEN SQUABBLING ABOUT THAT SUBJECT FOR A LONG TIME... IF THERE IS ONE, IT HAS TO BE VERY THIN...
WHAT IS YOUR OPINION, PROFESSOR?
THERE HAVE BEEN ALL SORTS OF THEORIES ABOUT THE MOON...
YOUR ATLAS SAYS THERE ARE SEAS ON THE MOON!
NOT REALLY. THE ANCIENTS THOUGHT THE DARK REGIONS WERE SEAS, A VIEW WE NOW KNOW TO BE FALSE, AT LEAST REGARDING THE VISIBLE SIDE...
FOR MY PART, I WOULD EXPECT TO FIND VOLCANIC ACTIVITY, AT LEAST. WE COULD CERTAINLY SEE AN ERUPTION FROM HERE. THERE MIGHT BE AN ATMOSPHERE AND PERHAPS EVEN CLOUDS...
HANSEN THOUGHT THAT EARTH'S GRAVITY HAD DEFORMED THE MOON, GIVING IT THE SHAPE OF AN EGG... WITH ALL THE AIR CONCENTRATED ON THE DARK SIDE...
ERATOSTHENES THOUGHT THAT THE CIRCULAR STRUCTURES WERE THE FORTIFICATIONS OF GIGANTIC CITIES...
SEA OF TRANQUILITY, LAKE OF DEATH, MARSH OF DECAY... THE MOON SOUNDS LIKE A FUNNY PLACE!

UNFORTUNATELY, WE WILL NOT SETTLE THESE QUESTIONS DURING OUR VOYAGE...

WE MUST RETURN DURING ANOTHER PHASE OF THE MOON WHEN THE SUN IS SHINING ON THE SIDE HIDDEN FROM EARTH...

WITH ALL DUE RESPECT, PROFESSOR, I'LL SKIP THE NEXT TRIP!

Mountains of implausible height and craters of immeasurable depth scarred the moon's surface.

Occasionally we glimpsed a flash of pallid light. Starlight reflected on ice or a lake? A meteor? Or just an optical illusion?

Would we ever know?

HANS! WAKE UP!

MMM?

IT'S ELEVEN O'CLOCK... TIME TO PREPARE FOR THE MANEUVER!

SERAPHIN, TO THE COCKPIT! I WILL BE IN THE OBSERVATION DOME! STRAP YOURSELVES IN TIGHTLY—EVEN THE DOG!

SOPHIE, HANS: YOU KNOW WHAT TO DO. THE SLIGHTEST ERROR ON THE ANGLE OF THE ENGINES...

...AND WELCOME TO THE HEART OF THE SUN!

LISTEN CAREFULLY, EVERYONE... WITHOUT A REGULATOR, THE ENGINES WILL DRAIN THE TRACE AMOUNT OF ELECTRICITY IN THE BATTERIES.

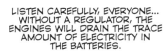

THERE WILL BE NO SECOND CHANCE!

READY?

FATHER!

WE SEEM TO BE LOSING ALTITUDE!

YOU'RE RIGHT!

MOREOVER, WE'RE ALSO SLIGHTLY OFF COURSE!

HOW CAN THAT BE?!

I DON'T KNOW! SINCE WE HAVE NOT ENGAGED THE ENGINES, AN EXTERNAL FORCE MUST BE ACTING UPON US!

LIKE A MAGNET?

THE AETHERSHIP IS ALUMINUM; IT'S NOT AFFECTED BY MAGNETISM... NO, I'M INCLINED TOWARD A GRAVITATIONAL ANOMALY...

LOOK!!

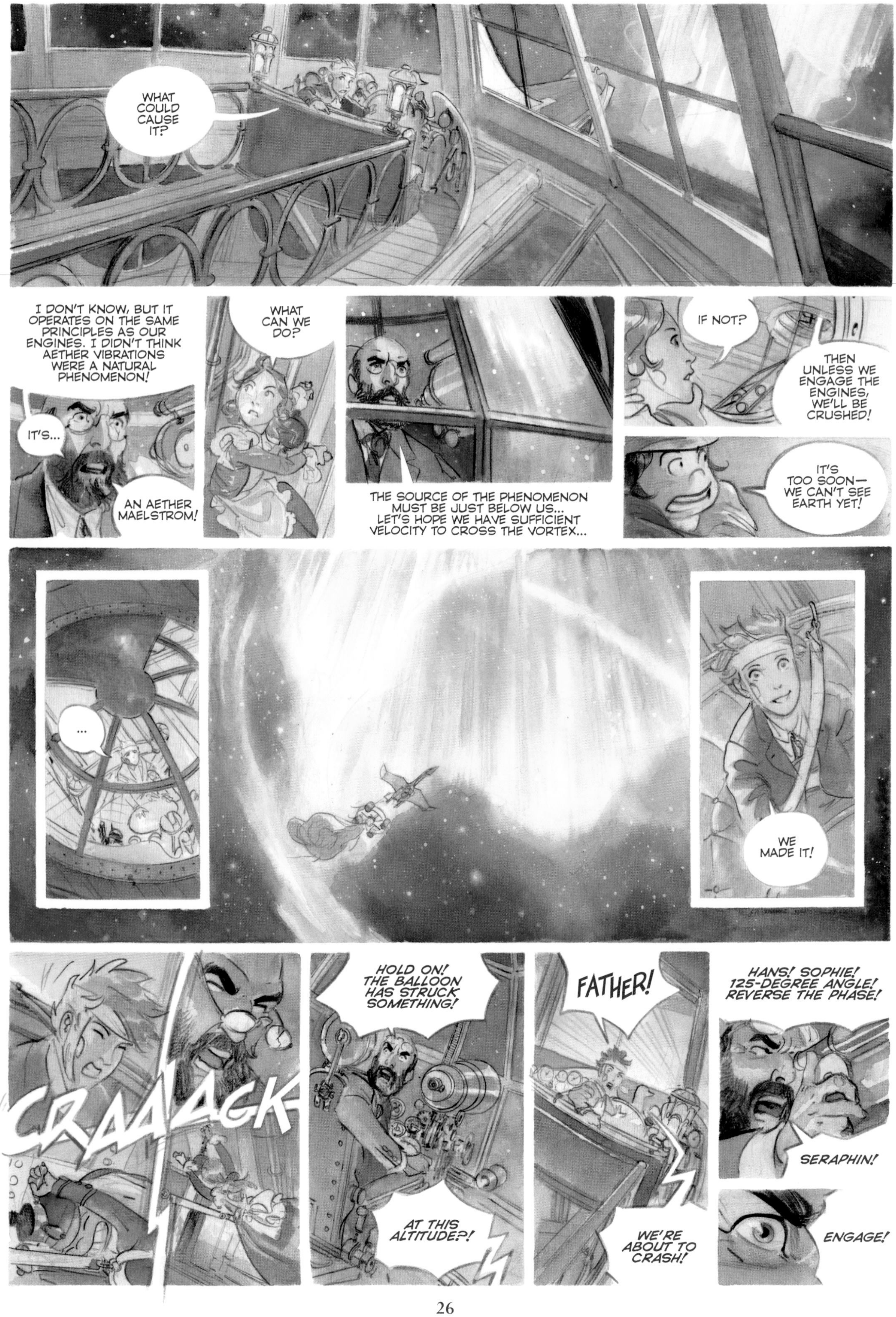
WHAT COULD CAUSE IT?
I DON'T KNOW, BUT IT OPERATES ON THE SAME PRINCIPLES AS OUR ENGINES. I DIDN'T THINK AETHER VIBRATIONS WERE A NATURAL PHENOMENON!
IT'S...
AN AETHER MAELSTROM!
WHAT CAN WE DO?
THE SOURCE OF THE PHENOMENON MUST BE JUST BELOW US... LET'S HOPE WE HAVE SUFFICIENT VELOCITY TO CROSS THE VORTEX...
IF NOT?
THEN UNLESS WE ENGAGE THE ENGINES, WE'LL BE CRUSHED!
IT'S TOO SOON— WE CAN'T SEE EARTH YET!
...
WE MADE IT!
CRAAACK
HOLD ON! THE BALLOON HAS STRUCK SOMETHING!
AT THIS ALTITUDE?!
FATHER!
WE'RE ABOUT TO CRASH!
HANS! SOPHIE! 125-DEGREE ANGLE! REVERSE THE PHASE!
SERAPHIN!
ENGAGE!

RAISE THE WINGS!

DEPLOY THE LANDING GEAR!

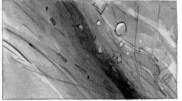

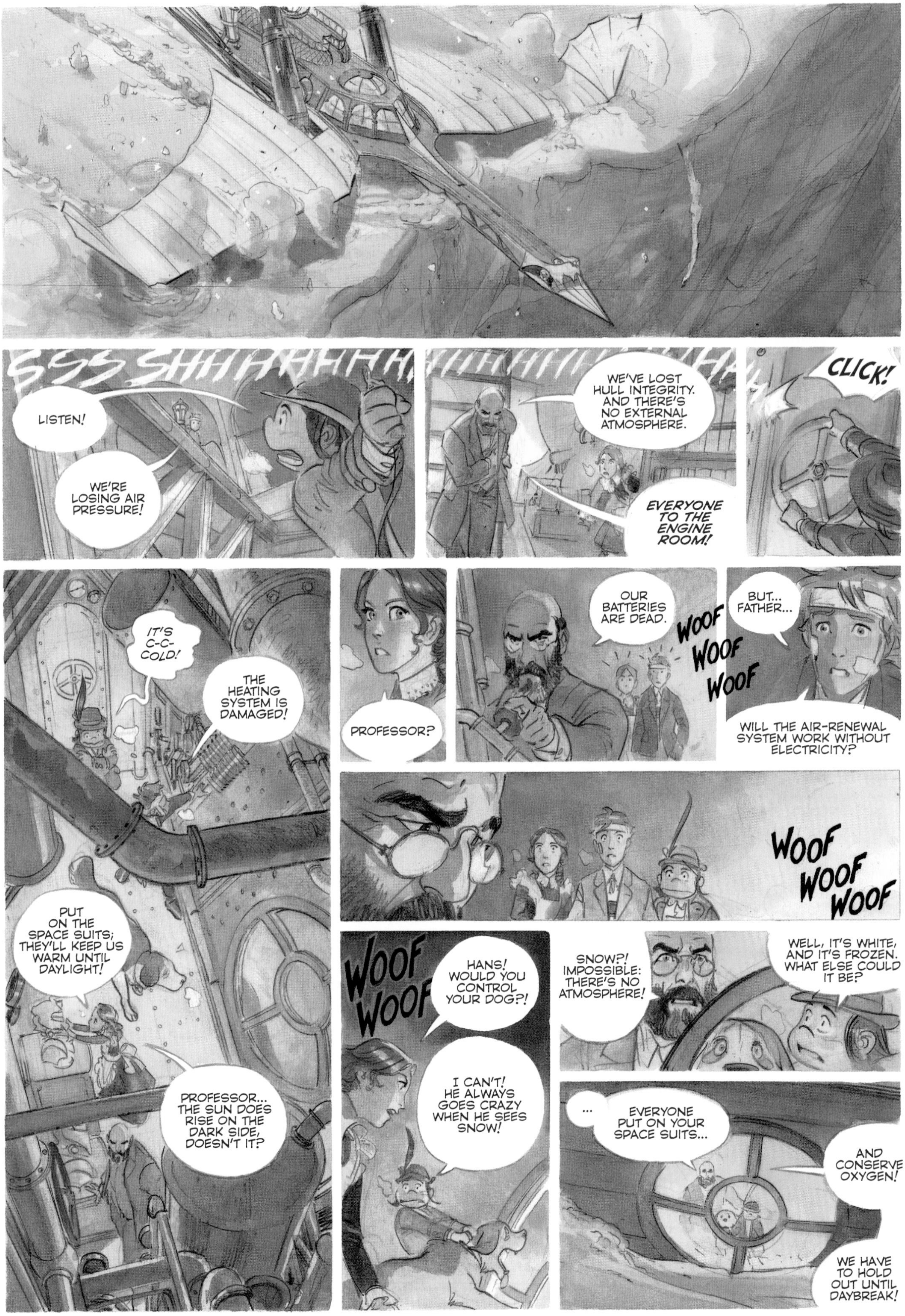
SSSSHHHHHHHHHHHHHHHHHHHHHHHHHHH
LISTEN!
WE'RE LOSING AIR PRESSURE!
WE'VE LOST HULL INTEGRITY. AND THERE'S NO EXTERNAL ATMOSPHERE.
EVERYONE TO THE ENGINE ROOM!
CLICK!
IT'S C-C-COLD!
THE HEATING SYSTEM IS DAMAGED!
PROFESSOR?
OUR BATTERIES ARE DEAD.
WOOF WOOF WOOF
BUT... FATHER...
WILL THE AIR-RENEWAL SYSTEM WORK WITHOUT ELECTRICITY?
PUT ON THE SPACE SUITS; THEY'LL KEEP US WARM UNTIL DAYLIGHT!
PROFESSOR... THE SUN DOES RISE ON THE DARK SIDE, DOESN'T IT?
WOOF WOOF WOOF
WOOF WOOF
HANS! WOULD YOU CONTROL YOUR DOG?!
I CAN'T! HE ALWAYS GOES CRAZY WHEN HE SEES SNOW!
SNOW?! IMPOSSIBLE: THERE'S NO ATMOSPHERE!
WELL, IT'S WHITE, AND IT'S FROZEN. WHAT ELSE COULD IT BE?
...
EVERYONE PUT ON YOUR SPACE SUITS...
AND CONSERVE OXYGEN!
WE HAVE TO HOLD OUT UNTIL DAYBREAK!

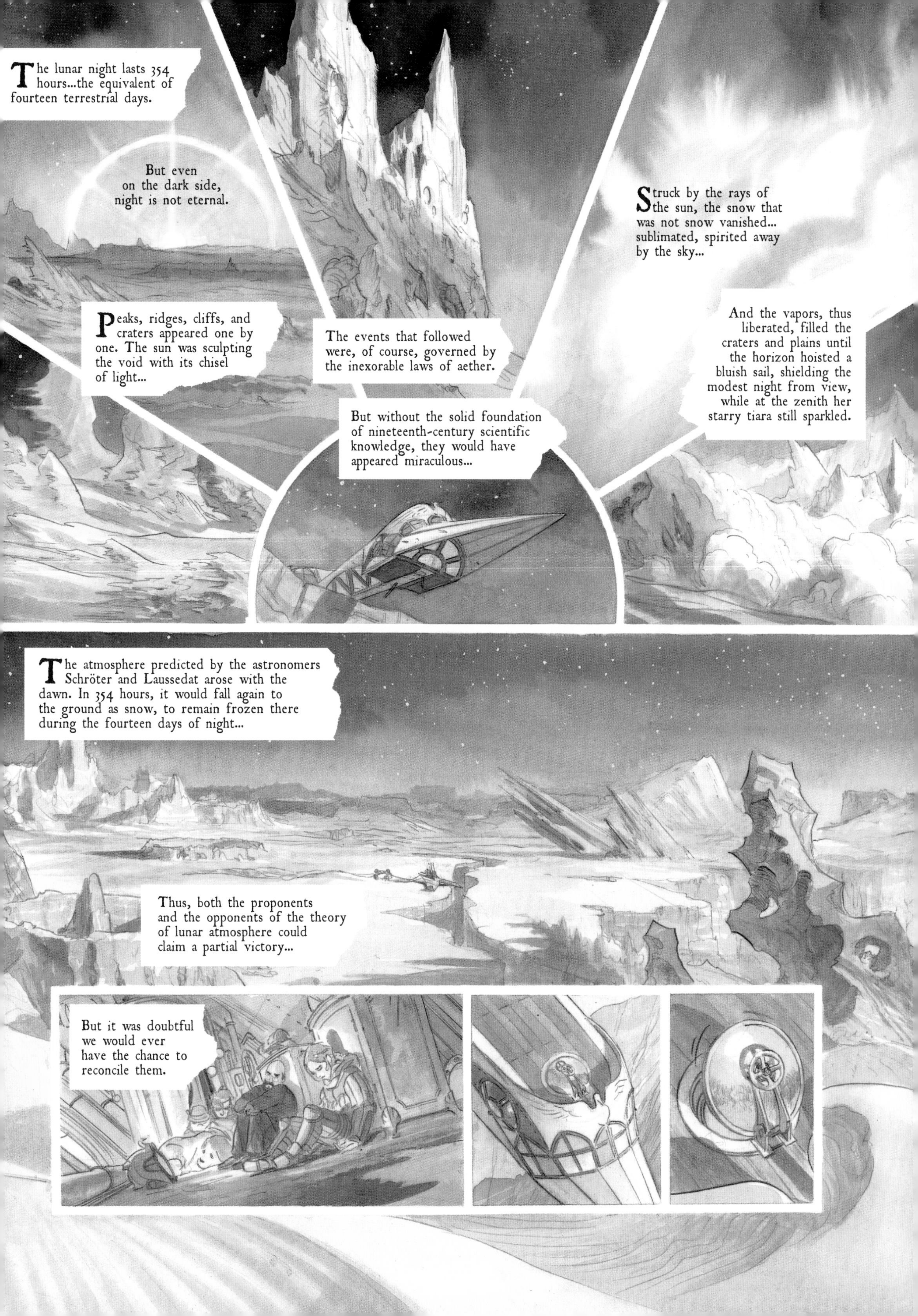
The lunar night lasts 354 hours...the equivalent of fourteen terrestrial days.
But even on the dark side, night is not eternal.
Peaks, ridges, cliffs, and craters appeared one by one. The sun was sculpting the void with its chisel of light...
The events that followed were, of course, governed by the inexorable laws of aether.
But without the solid foundation of nineteenth-century scientific knowledge, they would have appeared miraculous...
Struck by the rays of the sun, the snow that was not snow vanished... sublimated, spirited away by the sky...
And the vapors, thus liberated, filled the craters and plains until the horizon hoisted a bluish sail, shielding the modest night from view, while at the zenith her starry tiara still sparkled.
The atmosphere predicted by the astronomers Schröter and Laussedat arose with the dawn. In 354 hours, it would fall again to the ground as snow, to remain frozen there during the fourteen days of night...
Thus, both the proponents and the opponents of the theory of lunar atmosphere could claim a partial victory...
But it was doubtful we would ever have the chance to reconcile them.

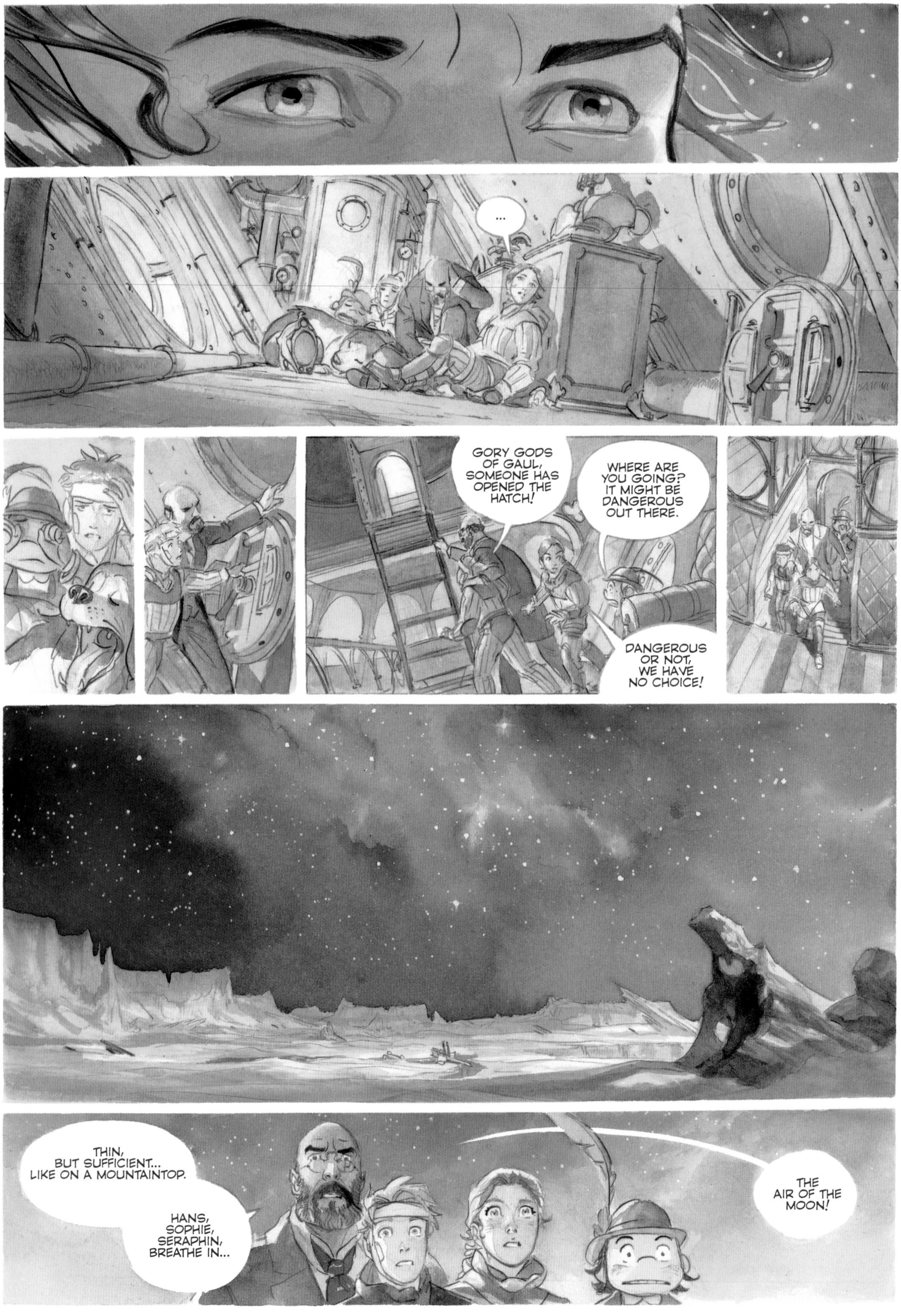
...
GORY GODS OF GAUL, SOMEONE HAS OPENED THE HATCH!
WHERE ARE YOU GOING? IT MIGHT BE DANGEROUS OUT THERE.
DANGEROUS OR NOT, WE HAVE NO CHOICE!
THE AIR OF THE MOON!
THIN, BUT SUFFICIENT... LIKE ON A MOUNTAINTOP.
HANS, SOPHIE, SERAPHIN, BREATHE IN...

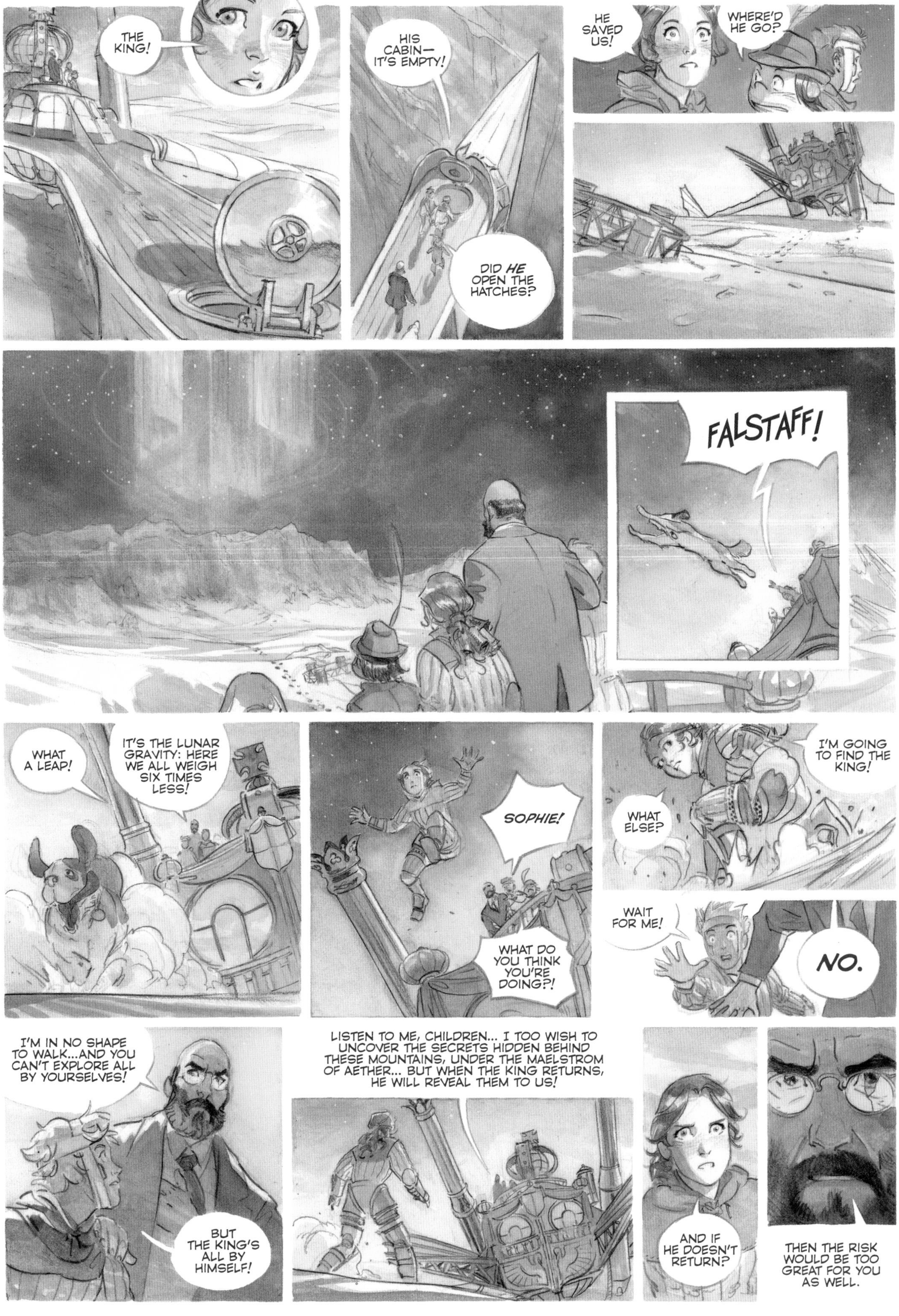
THE KING!
HIS CABIN— IT'S EMPTY!
DID HE OPEN THE HATCHES?
HE SAVED US!
WHERE'D HE GO?
FALSTAFF!
WHAT A LEAP!
IT'S THE LUNAR GRAVITY: HERE WE ALL WEIGH SIX TIMES LESS!
SOPHIE!
WHAT DO YOU THINK YOU'RE DOING?!
I'M GOING TO FIND THE KING!
WHAT ELSE?
WAIT FOR ME!
NO.
I'M IN NO SHAPE TO WALK...AND YOU CAN'T EXPLORE ALL BY YOURSELVES!
BUT THE KING'S ALL BY HIMSELF!
LISTEN TO ME, CHILDREN... I TOO WISH TO UNCOVER THE SECRETS HIDDEN BEHIND THESE MOUNTAINS, UNDER THE MAELSTROM OF AETHER... BUT WHEN THE KING RETURNS, HE WILL REVEAL THEM TO US!
AND IF HE DOESN'T RETURN?
THEN THE RISK WOULD BE TOO GREAT FOR YOU AS WELL.

I DON'T SEE HIM! HE MUST ALREADY BE IN THE MOUNTAINS...

SERAPHIN! SOPHIE! LET'S GO! WE HAVE 350 HOURS TO PREPARE THIS CRAFT FOR FLIGHT!

BUT PROFESSOR, WITHOUT A BALLOON AND A REGULATOR, IT'S IMPOSSIBLE!

THE BALLOON IS NOTHING BUT CANVAS! WE CAN REPAIR IT, AND WE STILL HAVE RESERVES OF HYDROGEN. AS FOR THE REGULATOR...

WE ARE THE CONQUERORS OF AETHER, ARE WE NOT?

BRING ALL THE ELECTRICAL COMPONENTS YOU CAN FIND UNDER THE RIGHT WING. WE MANAGED TO GET OURSELVES INTO THIS MESS; I REFUSE TO BELIEVE WE CAN'T GET OURSELVES OUT!

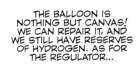

AH!

LOOK DOWN THERE!

WELL, WELL, WELL! A BICYCLE!

NOW WE KNOW THERE'S INTELLIGENT LIFE ON THE MOON!

EXCEPT IN YOUR CASE, HANS!

THAT'S YOUR PROTOTYPE, HANS! IT MUST HAVE BEEN WEDGED INTO THE PARAPET WHEN WE TOOK OFF!

WHAT DID YOU FIND THERE, OLD FELLOW?

WHAT IS THAT?

OH! IT'S A SHELL!

A FOSSIL!

WE MUST BE AT THE BOTTOM OF AN ANCIENT SEA, WHERE LIFE AROSE, EVOLVED...

AND THEN DISAPPEARED...

AROSE, SURE...

BUT HOW DO YOU KNOW IT DISAPPEARED?

We planned to divide the endless lunar day into fourteen terrestrial days: sixteen hours of work, eight hours of rest.

The first day was dedicated to setting up camp in the shadow of our great white bird.

Under the wing, the laboratory and a bunk for my father.

At the stern, quarters for the exhausted crew who were getting ready to spend their first night on the Moon...

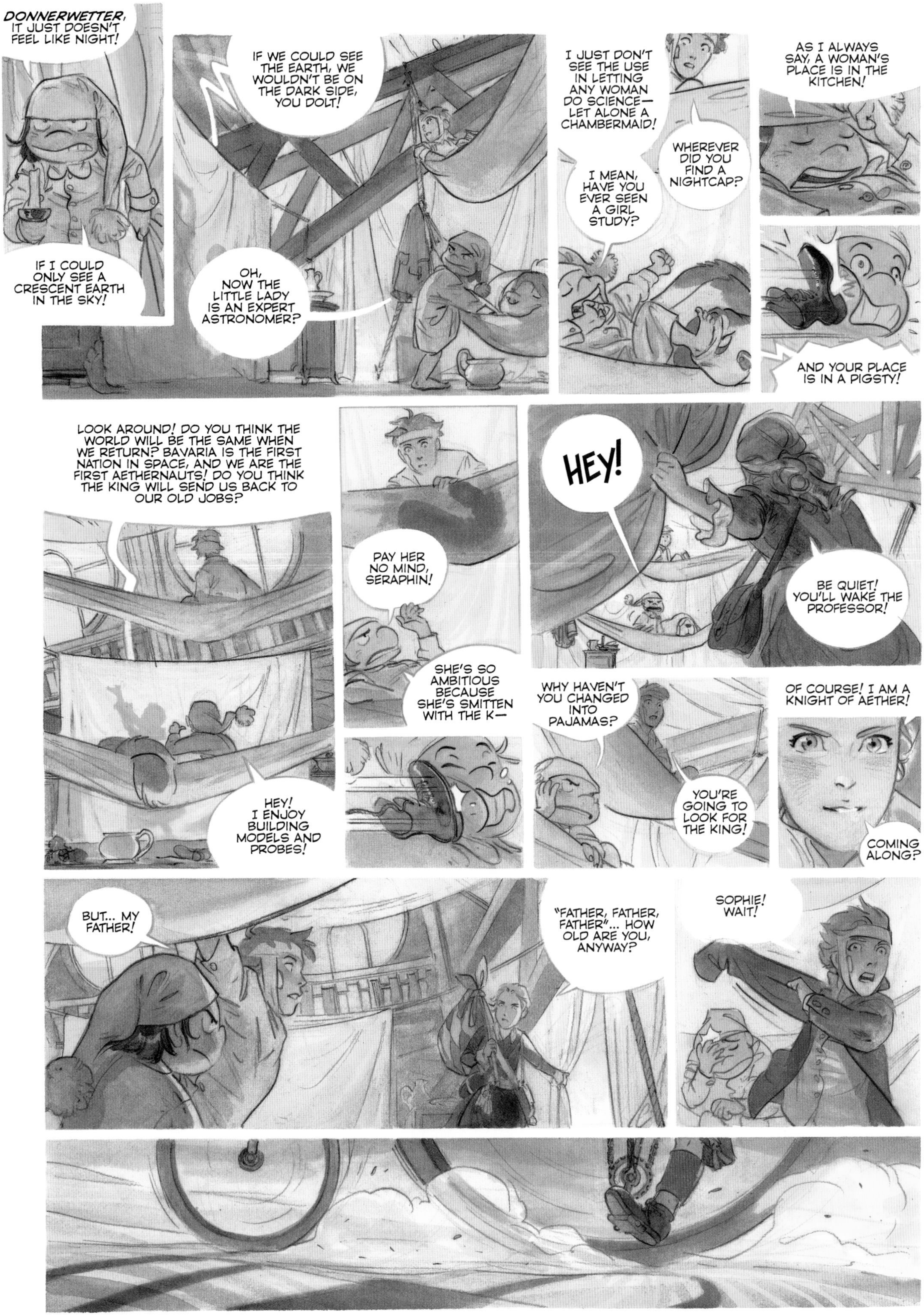

DONNERWETTER, IT JUST DOESN'T FEEL LIKE NIGHT!
IF I COULD ONLY SEE A CRESCENT EARTH IN THE SKY!
IF WE COULD SEE THE EARTH, WE WOULDN'T BE ON THE DARK SIDE, YOU DOLT!
OH, NOW THE LITTLE LADY IS AN EXPERT ASTRONOMER?
I JUST DON'T SEE THE USE IN LETTING ANY WOMAN DO SCIENCE—LET ALONE A CHAMBERMAID!
I MEAN, HAVE YOU EVER SEEN A GIRL STUDY?
WHEREVER DID YOU FIND A NIGHTCAP?
AS I ALWAYS SAY, A WOMAN'S PLACE IS IN THE KITCHEN!
AND YOUR PLACE IS IN A PIGSTY!
LOOK AROUND! DO YOU THINK THE WORLD WILL BE THE SAME WHEN WE RETURN? BAVARIA IS THE FIRST NATION IN SPACE, AND WE ARE THE FIRST AETHERNAUTS! DO YOU THINK THE KING WILL SEND US BACK TO OUR OLD JOBS?
HEY! I ENJOY BUILDING MODELS AND PROBES!
PAY HER NO MIND, SERAPHIN!
SHE'S SO AMBITIOUS BECAUSE SHE'S SMITTEN WITH THE K—
HEY!
BE QUIET! YOU'LL WAKE THE PROFESSOR!
WHY HAVEN'T YOU CHANGED INTO PAJAMAS?
YOU'RE GOING TO LOOK FOR THE KING!
OF COURSE! I AM A KNIGHT OF AETHER!
COMING ALONG?
BUT... MY FATHER!
"FATHER, FATHER, FATHER"... HOW OLD ARE YOU, ANYWAY?
SOPHIE! WAIT!

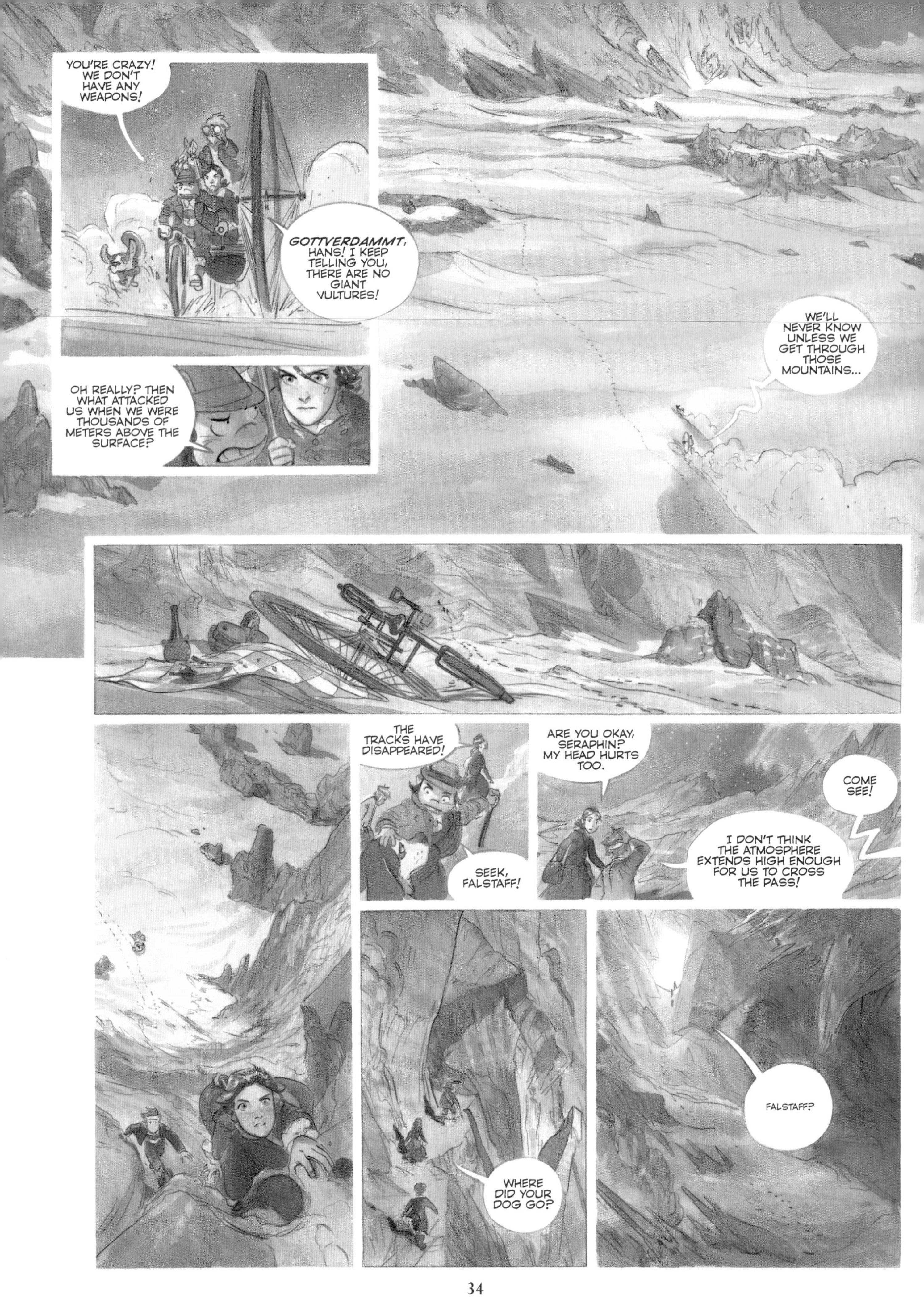

YOU'RE CRAZY! WE DON'T HAVE ANY WEAPONS!
GOTTVERDAMMT, HANS! I KEEP TELLING YOU, THERE ARE NO GIANT VULTURES!
OH REALLY? THEN WHAT ATTACKED US WHEN WE WERE THOUSANDS OF METERS ABOVE THE SURFACE?
WE'LL NEVER KNOW UNLESS WE GET THROUGH THOSE MOUNTAINS...
THE TRACKS HAVE DISAPPEARED!
SEEK, FALSTAFF!
ARE YOU OKAY, SERAPHIN? MY HEAD HURTS TOO.
COME SEE!
I DON'T THINK THE ATMOSPHERE EXTENDS HIGH ENOUGH FOR US TO CROSS THE PASS!
WHERE DID YOUR DOG GO?
FALSTAFF?

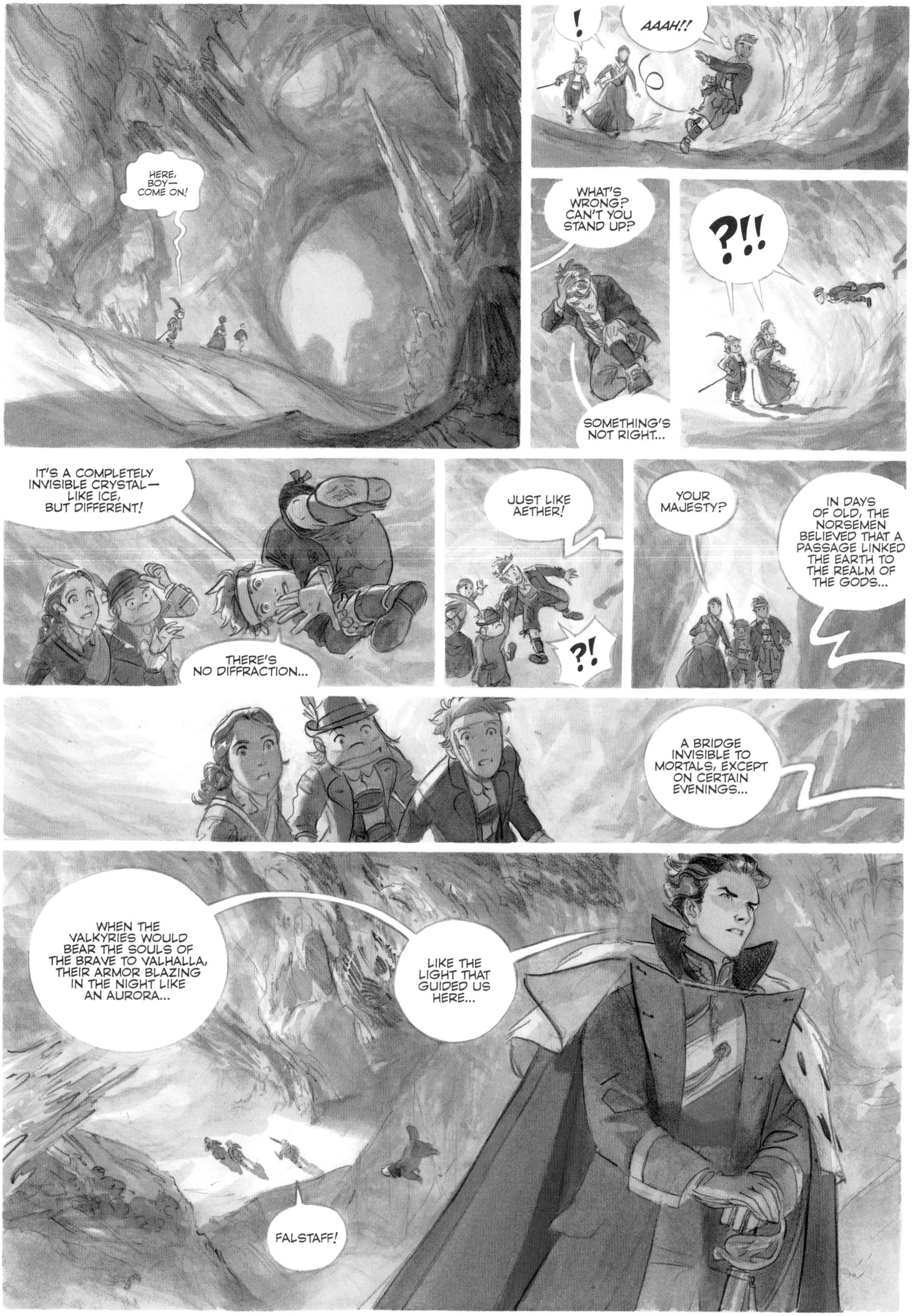

HERE, BOY— COME ON!
!
AAAH!!
WHAT'S WRONG? CAN'T YOU STAND UP?
SOMETHING'S NOT RIGHT...
?!!
IT'S A COMPLETELY INVISIBLE CRYSTAL— LIKE ICE, BUT DIFFERENT!
THERE'S NO DIFFRACTION...
JUST LIKE AETHER!
?!
YOUR MAJESTY?
IN DAYS OF OLD, THE NORSEMEN BELIEVED THAT A PASSAGE LINKED THE EARTH TO THE REALM OF THE GODS...
A BRIDGE INVISIBLE TO MORTALS, EXCEPT ON CERTAIN EVENINGS...
WHEN THE VALKYRIES WOULD BEAR THE SOULS OF THE BRAVE TO VALHALLA, THEIR ARMOR BLAZING IN THE NIGHT LIKE AN AURORA...
LIKE THE LIGHT THAT GUIDED US HERE...
FALSTAFF!

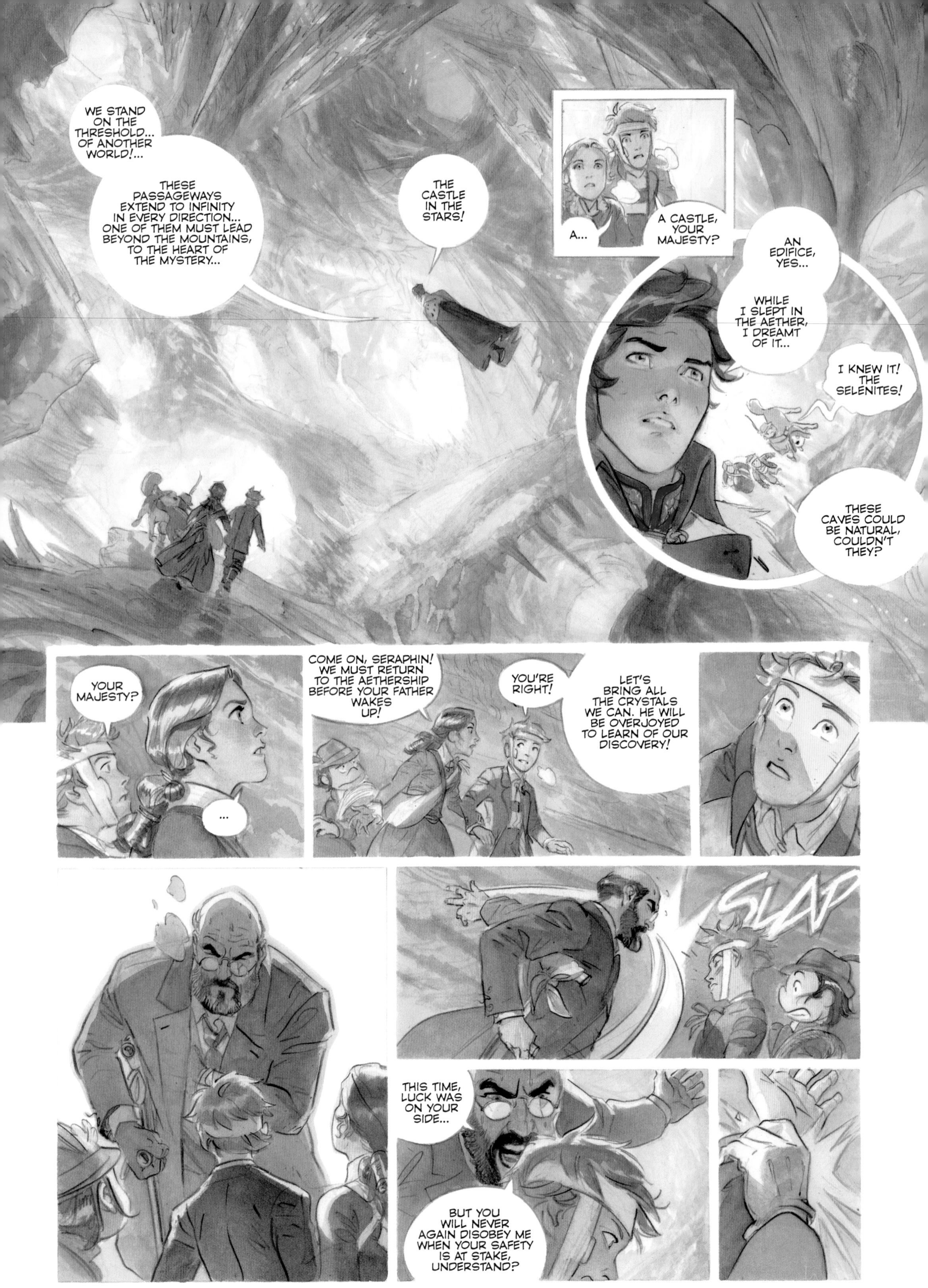
WE STAND ON THE THRESHOLD... OF ANOTHER WORLD!...
THESE PASSAGEWAYS EXTEND TO INFINITY IN EVERY DIRECTION... ONE OF THEM MUST LEAD BEYOND THE MOUNTAINS, TO THE HEART OF THE MYSTERY...
THE CASTLE IN THE STARS!
A...
A CASTLE, YOUR MAJESTY?
AN EDIFICE, YES...
WHILE I SLEPT IN THE AETHER, I DREAMT OF IT...
I KNEW IT! THE SELENITES!
THESE CAVES COULD BE NATURAL, COULDN'T THEY?
YOUR MAJESTY?
...
COME ON, SERAPHIN! WE MUST RETURN TO THE AETHERSHIP BEFORE YOUR FATHER WAKES UP!
YOU'RE RIGHT!
LET'S BRING ALL THE CRYSTALS WE CAN. HE WILL BE OVERJOYED TO LEARN OF OUR DISCOVERY!
SLAP
THIS TIME, LUCK WAS ON YOUR SIDE...
BUT YOU WILL NEVER AGAIN DISOBEY ME WHEN YOUR SAFETY IS AT STAKE, UNDERSTAND?

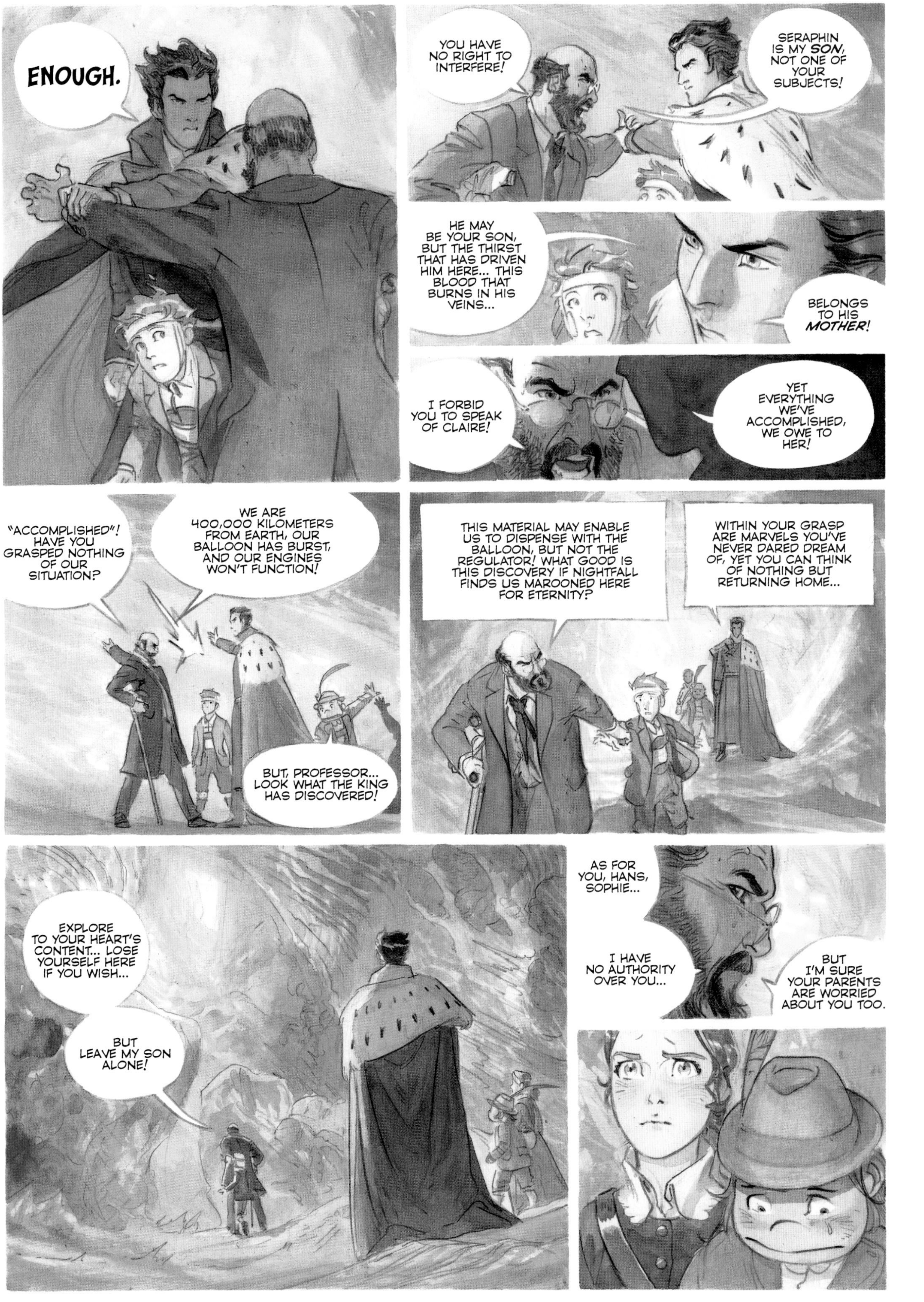
ENOUGH.
YOU HAVE NO RIGHT TO INTERFERE!
SERAPHIN IS MY SON, NOT ONE OF YOUR SUBJECTS!
HE MAY BE YOUR SON, BUT THE THIRST THAT HAS DRIVEN HIM HERE... THIS BLOOD THAT BURNS IN HIS VEINS...
BELONGS TO HIS MOTHER!
I FORBID YOU TO SPEAK OF CLAIRE!
YET EVERYTHING WE'VE ACCOMPLISHED, WE OWE TO HER!
"ACCOMPLISHED"! HAVE YOU GRASPED NOTHING OF OUR SITUATION?
WE ARE 400,000 KILOMETERS FROM EARTH, OUR BALLOON HAS BURST, AND OUR ENGINES WON'T FUNCTION!
BUT, PROFESSOR... LOOK WHAT THE KING HAS DISCOVERED!
THIS MATERIAL MAY ENABLE US TO DISPENSE WITH THE BALLOON, BUT NOT THE REGULATOR! WHAT GOOD IS THIS DISCOVERY IF NIGHTFALL FINDS US MAROONED HERE FOR ETERNITY?
WITHIN YOUR GRASP ARE MARVELS YOU'VE NEVER DARED DREAM OF, YET YOU CAN THINK OF NOTHING BUT RETURNING HOME...
EXPLORE TO YOUR HEART'S CONTENT... LOSE YOURSELF HERE IF YOU WISH...
BUT LEAVE MY SON ALONE!
AS FOR YOU, HANS, SOPHIE...
I HAVE NO AUTHORITY OVER YOU...
BUT I'M SURE YOUR PARENTS ARE WORRIED ABOUT YOU TOO.

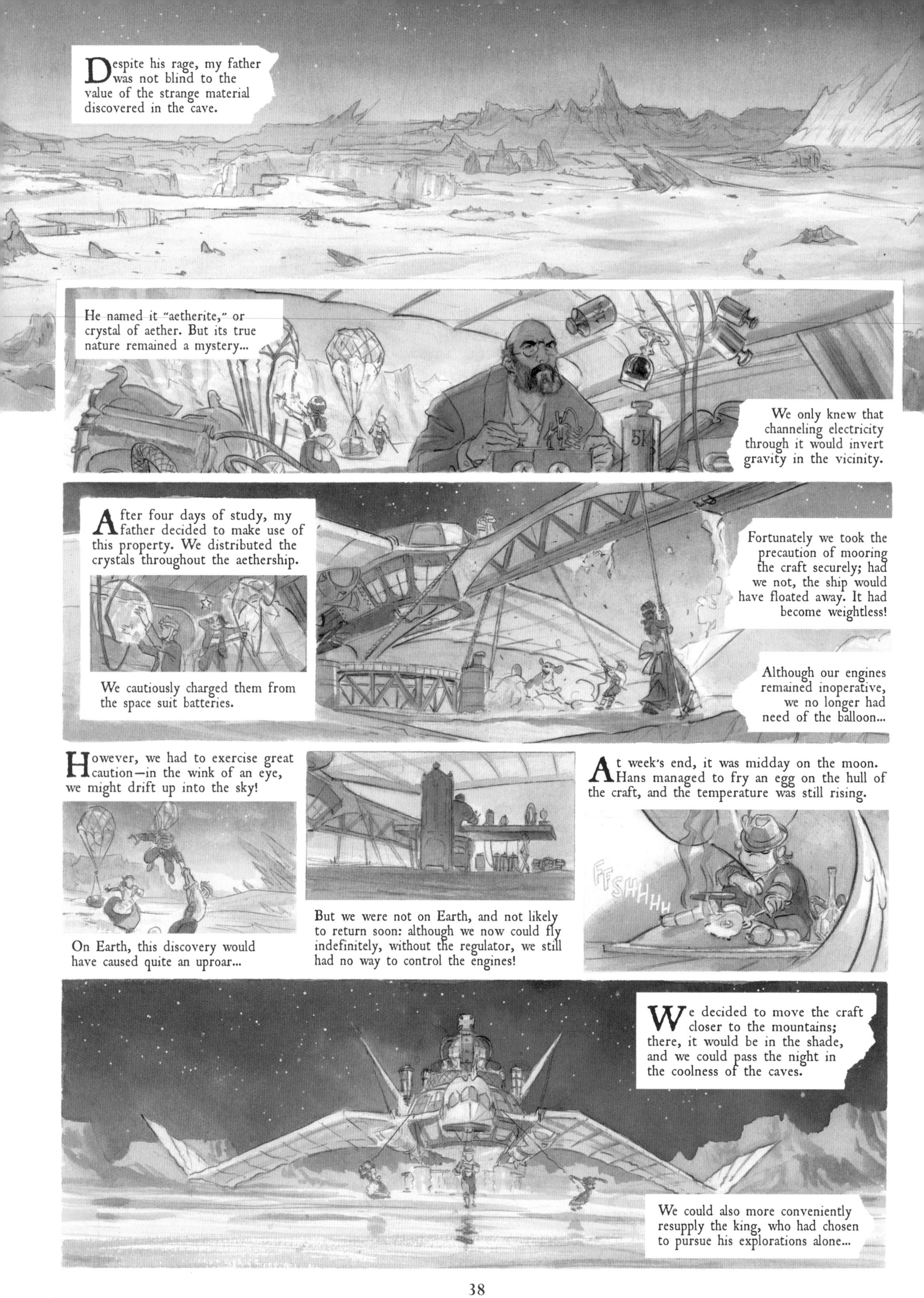
Despite his rage, my father was not blind to the value of the strange material discovered in the cave.
He named it "aetherite," or crystal of aether. But its true nature remained a mystery...
We only knew that channeling electricity through it would invert gravity in the vicinity.
51
After four days of study, my father decided to make use of this property. We distributed the crystals throughout the aethership.
We cautiously charged them from the space suit batteries.
Fortunately we took the precaution of mooring the craft securely; had we not, the ship would have floated away. It had become weightless!
Although our engines remained inoperative, we no longer had need of the balloon...
However, we had to exercise great caution—in the wink of an eye, we might drift up into the sky!
On Earth, this discovery would have caused quite an uproar...
But we were not on Earth, and not likely to return soon: although we now could fly indefinitely, without the regulator, we still had no way to control the engines!
At week's end, it was midday on the moon. Hans managed to fry an egg on the hull of the craft, and the temperature was still rising.
FFSHHHH
We decided to move the craft closer to the mountains; there, it would be in the shade, and we could pass the night in the coolness of the caves.
We could also more conveniently resupply the king, who had chosen to pursue his explorations alone...

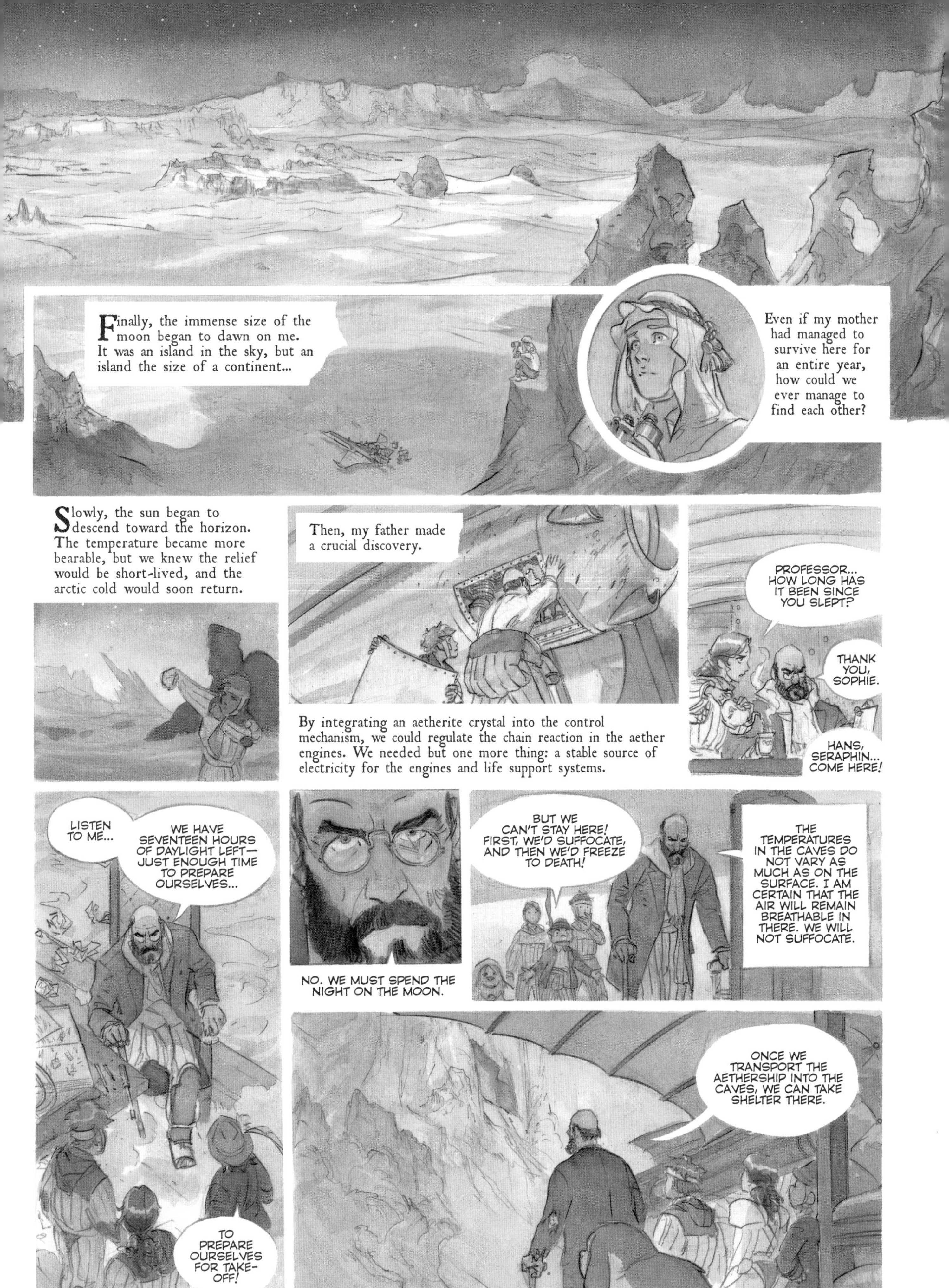

Finally, the immense size of the moon began to dawn on me. It was an island in the sky, but an island the size of a continent...
Even if my mother had managed to survive here for an entire year, how could we ever manage to find each other?
Slowly, the sun began to descend toward the horizon. The temperature became more bearable, but we knew the relief would be short-lived, and the arctic cold would soon return.
Then, my father made a crucial discovery.
By integrating an aetherite crystal into the control mechanism, we could regulate the chain reaction in the aether engines. We needed but one more thing: a stable source of electricity for the engines and life support systems.
PROFESSOR... HOW LONG HAS IT BEEN SINCE YOU SLEPT?
THANK YOU, SOPHIE.
HANS, SERAPHIN... COME HERE!
LISTEN TO ME...
WE HAVE SEVENTEEN HOURS OF DAYLIGHT LEFT— JUST ENOUGH TIME TO PREPARE OURSELVES...
TO PREPARE OURSELVES FOR TAKE-OFF!
NO. WE MUST SPEND THE NIGHT ON THE MOON.
BUT WE CAN'T STAY HERE! FIRST, WE'D SUFFOCATE, AND THEN WE'D FREEZE TO DEATH!
THE TEMPERATURES IN THE CAVES DO NOT VARY AS MUCH AS ON THE SURFACE. I AM CERTAIN THAT THE AIR WILL REMAIN BREATHABLE IN THERE. WE WILL NOT SUFFOCATE.
ONCE WE TRANSPORT THE AETHERSHIP INTO THE CAVES, WE CAN TAKE SHELTER THERE.

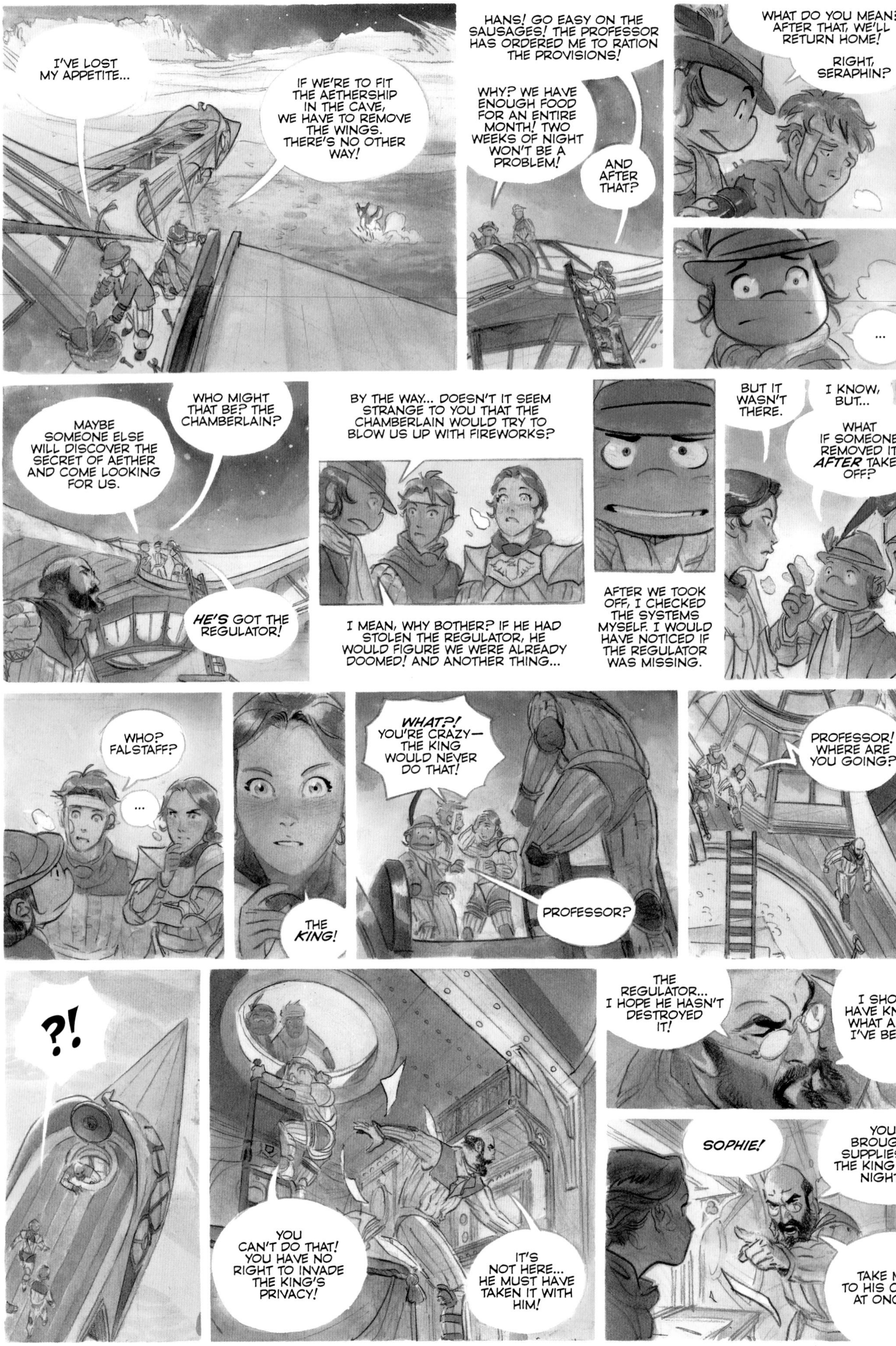
I'VE LOST MY APPETITE...
IF WE'RE TO FIT THE AETHERSHIP IN THE CAVE, WE HAVE TO REMOVE THE WINGS. THERE'S NO OTHER WAY!
HANS! GO EASY ON THE SAUSAGES! THE PROFESSOR HAS ORDERED ME TO RATION THE PROVISIONS!
WHY? WE HAVE ENOUGH FOOD FOR AN ENTIRE MONTH! TWO WEEKS OF NIGHT WON'T BE A PROBLEM!
AND AFTER THAT?
WHAT DO YOU MEAN? AFTER THAT, WE'LL RETURN HOME!
RIGHT, SERAPHIN?
...
MAYBE SOMEONE ELSE WILL DISCOVER THE SECRET OF AETHER AND COME LOOKING FOR US.
WHO MIGHT THAT BE? THE CHAMBERLAIN?
HE'S GOT THE REGULATOR!
BY THE WAY... DOESN'T IT SEEM STRANGE TO YOU THAT THE CHAMBERLAIN WOULD TRY TO BLOW US UP WITH FIREWORKS?
I MEAN, WHY BOTHER? IF HE HAD STOLEN THE REGULATOR, HE WOULD FIGURE WE WERE ALREADY DOOMED! AND ANOTHER THING...
AFTER WE TOOK OFF, I CHECKED THE SYSTEMS MYSELF. I WOULD HAVE NOTICED IF THE REGULATOR WAS MISSING.
BUT IT WASN'T THERE.
I KNOW, BUT...
WHAT IF SOMEONE REMOVED IT AFTER TAKE-OFF?
WHO? FALSTAFF?
...
THE KING!
WHAT?! YOU'RE CRAZY—THE KING WOULD NEVER DO THAT!
PROFESSOR?
PROFESSOR! WHERE ARE YOU GOING?
?!
YOU CAN'T DO THAT! YOU HAVE NO RIGHT TO INVADE THE KING'S PRIVACY!
IT'S NOT HERE... HE MUST HAVE TAKEN IT WITH HIM!
THE REGULATOR... I HOPE HE HASN'T DESTROYED IT!
I SHOULD HAVE KNOWN! WHAT A FOOL I'VE BEEN!...
SOPHIE!
YOU BROUGHT SUPPLIES TO THE KING LAST NIGHT!
TAKE ME TO HIS CAMP AT ONCE!

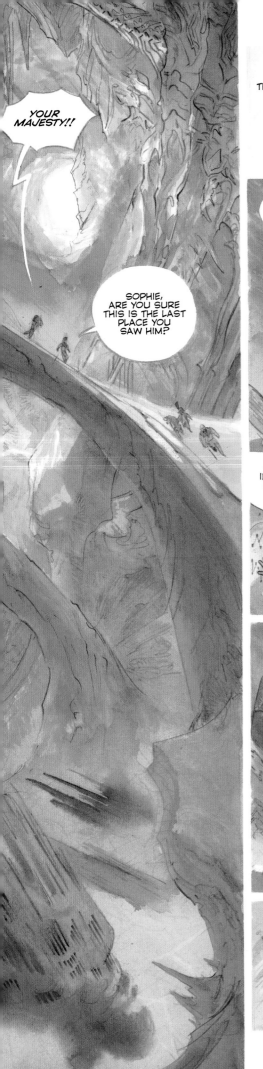

YOUR MAJESTY!!

SOPHIE, ARE YOU SURE THIS IS THE LAST PLACE YOU SAW HIM?

I THINK SO... BUT THESE TUNNELS ARE SUCH A MAZE!

YOUR MAJESTY!

FALSTAFF! FIND THE KING!

THIS WAY!

PILLARS!

DONNERWETTER! A SELENITE TEMPLE!

VOLCANIC FORMATIONS, LIKE THE GIANT'S CAUSEWAY IN IRELAND. THE ANCIENTS THOUGHT THEY WERE BUILT BY THE GODS. WE MUST NOT MAKE THE SAME MISTAKE!

NO— THESE ARE NATURAL FORMATIONS!

?

SO ALL THIS IS NATURAL! INCREDIBLE! LOOK AT THIS! IF I DIDN'T KNOW BETTER, I'D THINK THIS WAS WRITING!

!?

...

I'M FAMILIAR WITH CALCITE PEARLS AND PYRITE NODULES, BUT THEY'RE NOT PERFECT SPHERES!

WELL, THIS ONE ISN'T A PERFECT SPHERE, EITHER! IT HAS SMALL CRATERS, LIKE...

OVER HERE!

PROFESSOR?

DO SPHERES LIKE THIS OCCUR IN NATURE?

THESE AREN'T NATURAL FORMATIONS...

THEY'RE A MODEL!

CHAPTER 6
THE MOON-KING

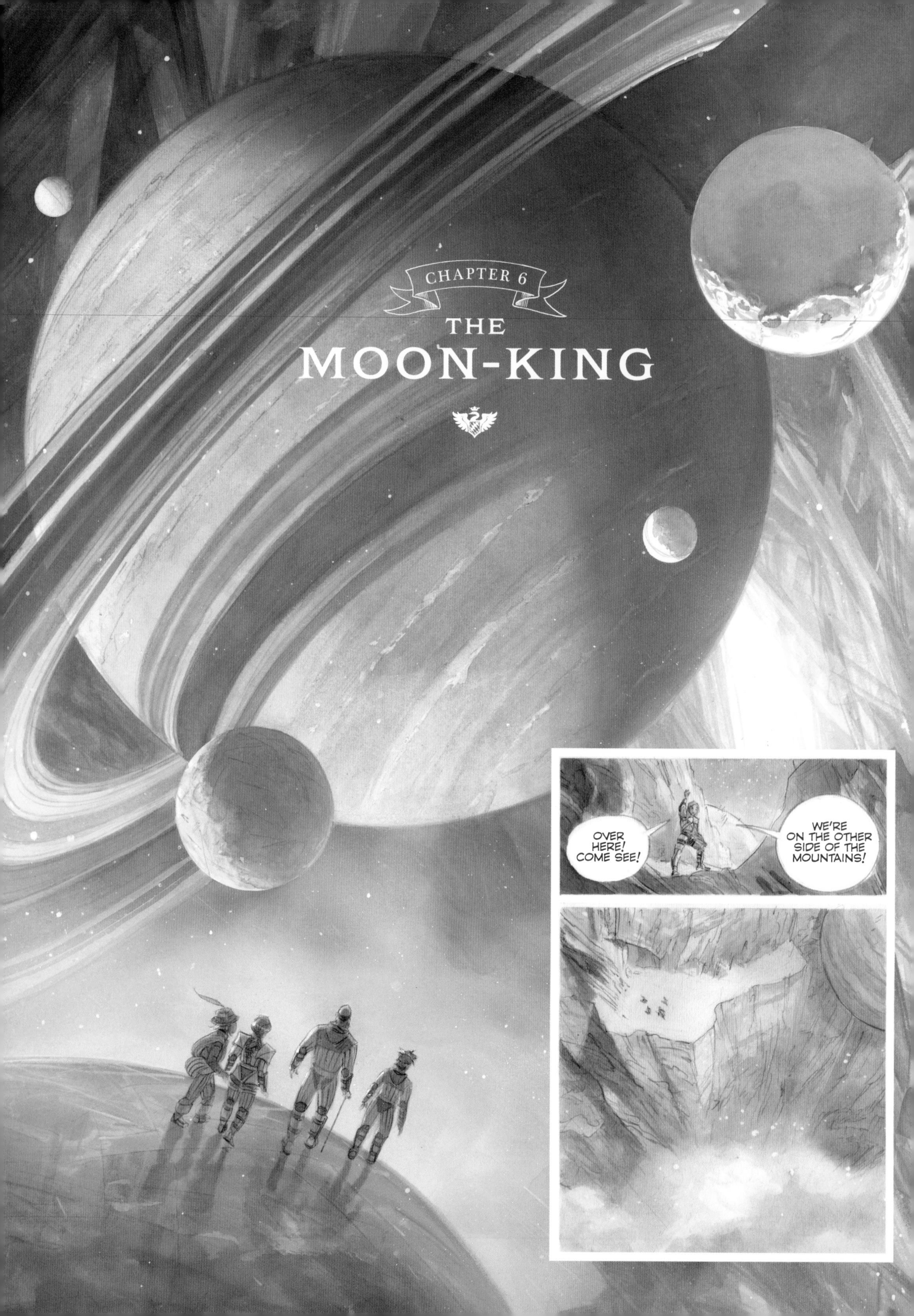
OVER HERE! COME SEE!
WE'RE ON THE OTHER SIDE OF THE MOUNTAINS!

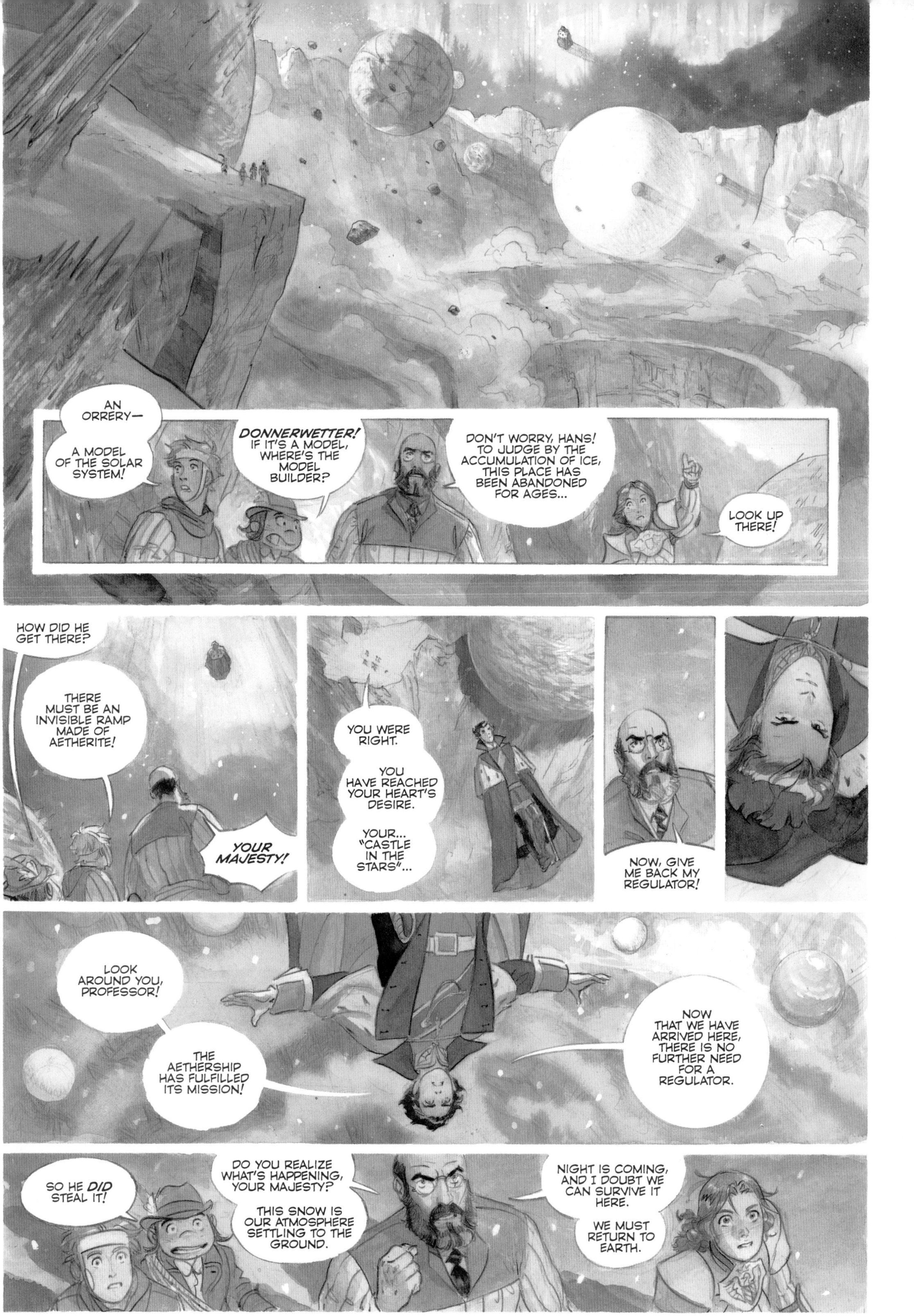
AN ORRERY—
A MODEL OF THE SOLAR SYSTEM!
DONNERWETTER! IF IT'S A MODEL, WHERE'S THE MODEL BUILDER?
DON'T WORRY, HANS! TO JUDGE BY THE ACCUMULATION OF ICE, THIS PLACE HAS BEEN ABANDONED FOR AGES...
LOOK UP THERE!
HOW DID HE GET THERE?
THERE MUST BE AN INVISIBLE RAMP MADE OF AETHERITE!
YOUR MAJESTY!
YOU WERE RIGHT.
YOU HAVE REACHED YOUR HEART'S DESIRE.
YOUR... "CASTLE IN THE STARS"...
NOW, GIVE ME BACK MY REGULATOR!
LOOK AROUND YOU, PROFESSOR!
THE AETHERSHIP HAS FULFILLED ITS MISSION!
NOW THAT WE HAVE ARRIVED HERE, THERE IS NO FURTHER NEED FOR A REGULATOR.
SO HE DID STEAL IT!
DO YOU REALIZE WHAT'S HAPPENING, YOUR MAJESTY?
THIS SNOW IS OUR ATMOSPHERE SETTLING TO THE GROUND.
NIGHT IS COMING, AND I DOUBT WE CAN SURVIVE IT HERE.
WE MUST RETURN TO EARTH.

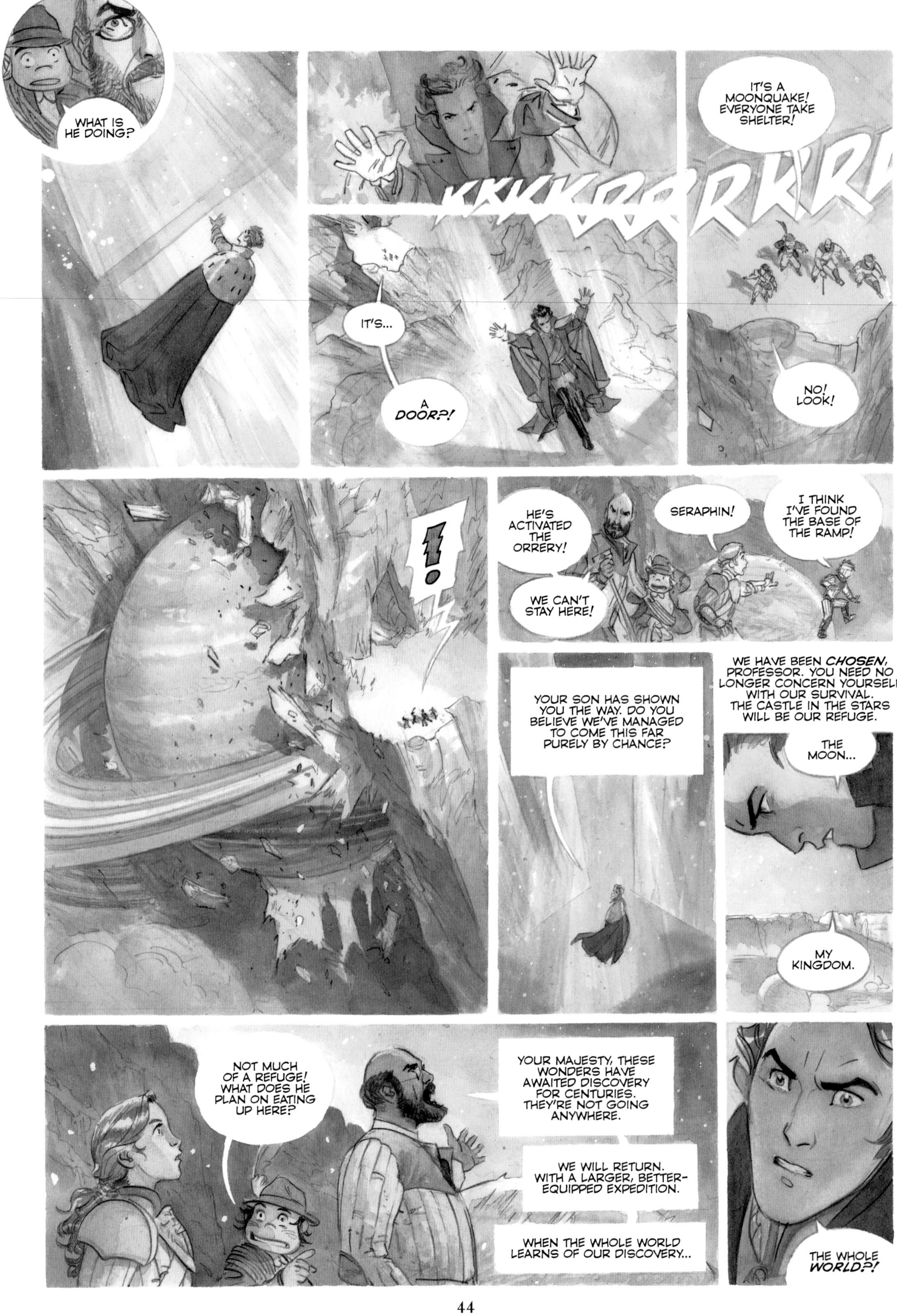

WHAT IS HE DOING?
IT'S A MOONQUAKE! EVERYONE TAKE SHELTER!
KKKKRRRRRKRR
IT'S...
A *DOOR?!*
NO! LOOK!
!
HE'S ACTIVATED THE ORRERY!
WE CAN'T STAY HERE!
SERAPHIN!
I THINK I'VE FOUND THE BASE OF THE RAMP!
YOUR SON HAS SHOWN YOU THE WAY. DO YOU BELIEVE WE'VE MANAGED TO COME THIS FAR PURELY BY CHANCE?
WE HAVE BEEN *CHOSEN*, PROFESSOR. YOU NEED NO LONGER CONCERN YOURSELF WITH OUR SURVIVAL. THE CASTLE IN THE STARS WILL BE OUR REFUGE.
THE MOON...
MY KINGDOM.
NOT MUCH OF A REFUGE! WHAT DOES HE PLAN ON EATING UP HERE?
YOUR MAJESTY, THESE WONDERS HAVE AWAITED DISCOVERY FOR CENTURIES. THEY'RE NOT GOING ANYWHERE.
WE WILL RETURN. WITH A LARGER, BETTER-EQUIPPED EXPEDITION.
WHEN THE WHOLE WORLD LEARNS OF OUR DISCOVERY...
THE WHOLE *WORLD?!*

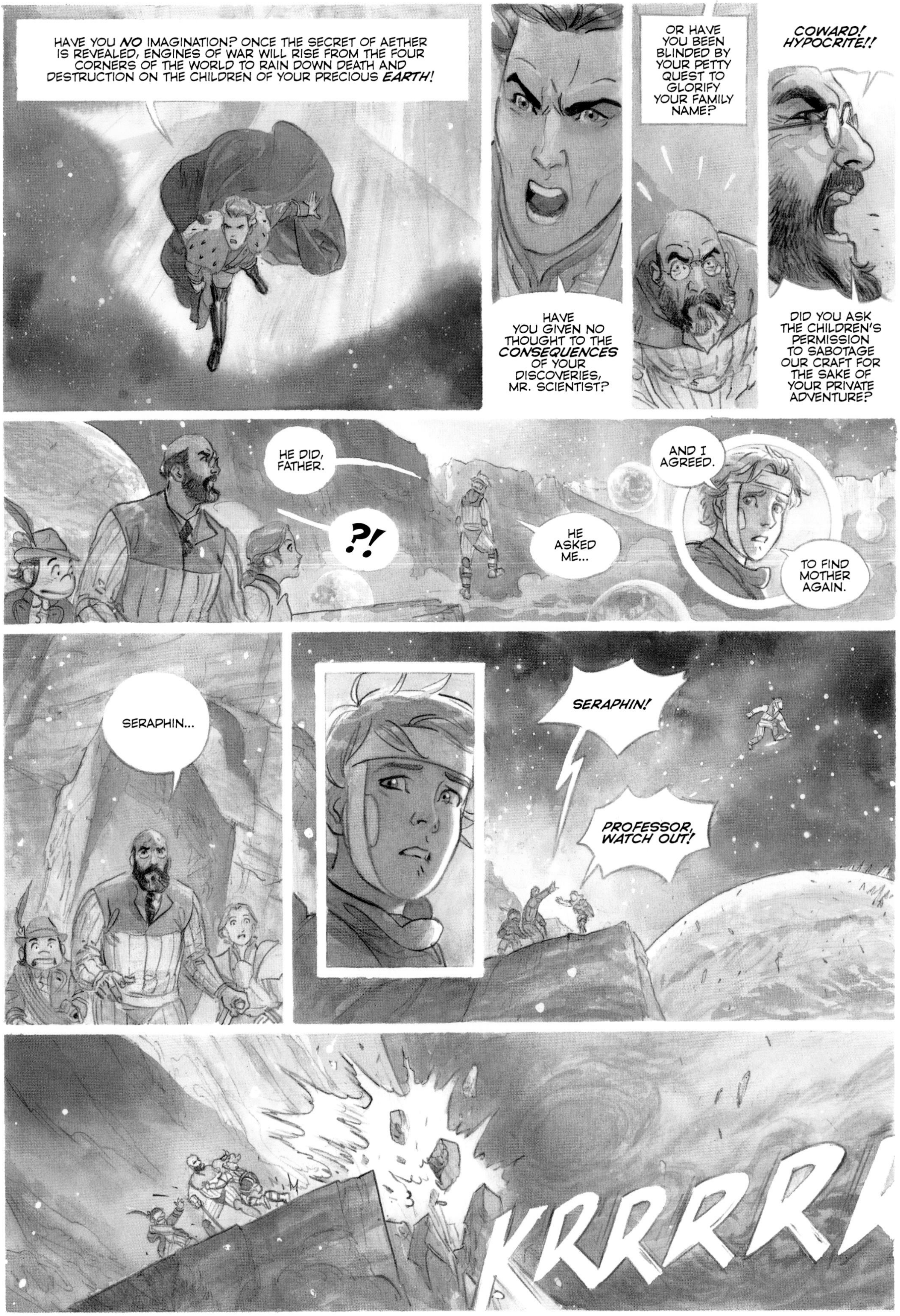
HAVE YOU **NO** IMAGINATION? ONCE THE SECRET OF AETHER IS REVEALED, ENGINES OF WAR WILL RISE FROM THE FOUR CORNERS OF THE WORLD TO RAIN DOWN DEATH AND DESTRUCTION ON THE CHILDREN OF YOUR PRECIOUS ***EARTH***!
HAVE YOU GIVEN NO THOUGHT TO THE ***CONSEQUENCES*** OF YOUR DISCOVERIES, MR. SCIENTIST?
OR HAVE YOU BEEN BLINDED BY YOUR PETTY QUEST TO GLORIFY YOUR FAMILY NAME?
COWARD! HYPOCRITE!!
DID YOU ASK THE CHILDREN'S PERMISSION TO SABOTAGE OUR CRAFT FOR THE SAKE OF YOUR PRIVATE ADVENTURE?
HE DID, FATHER.
?!
HE ASKED ME...
AND I AGREED.
TO FIND MOTHER AGAIN.
SERAPHIN...
SERAPHIN!
PROFESSOR, WATCH OUT!
KRRRRR

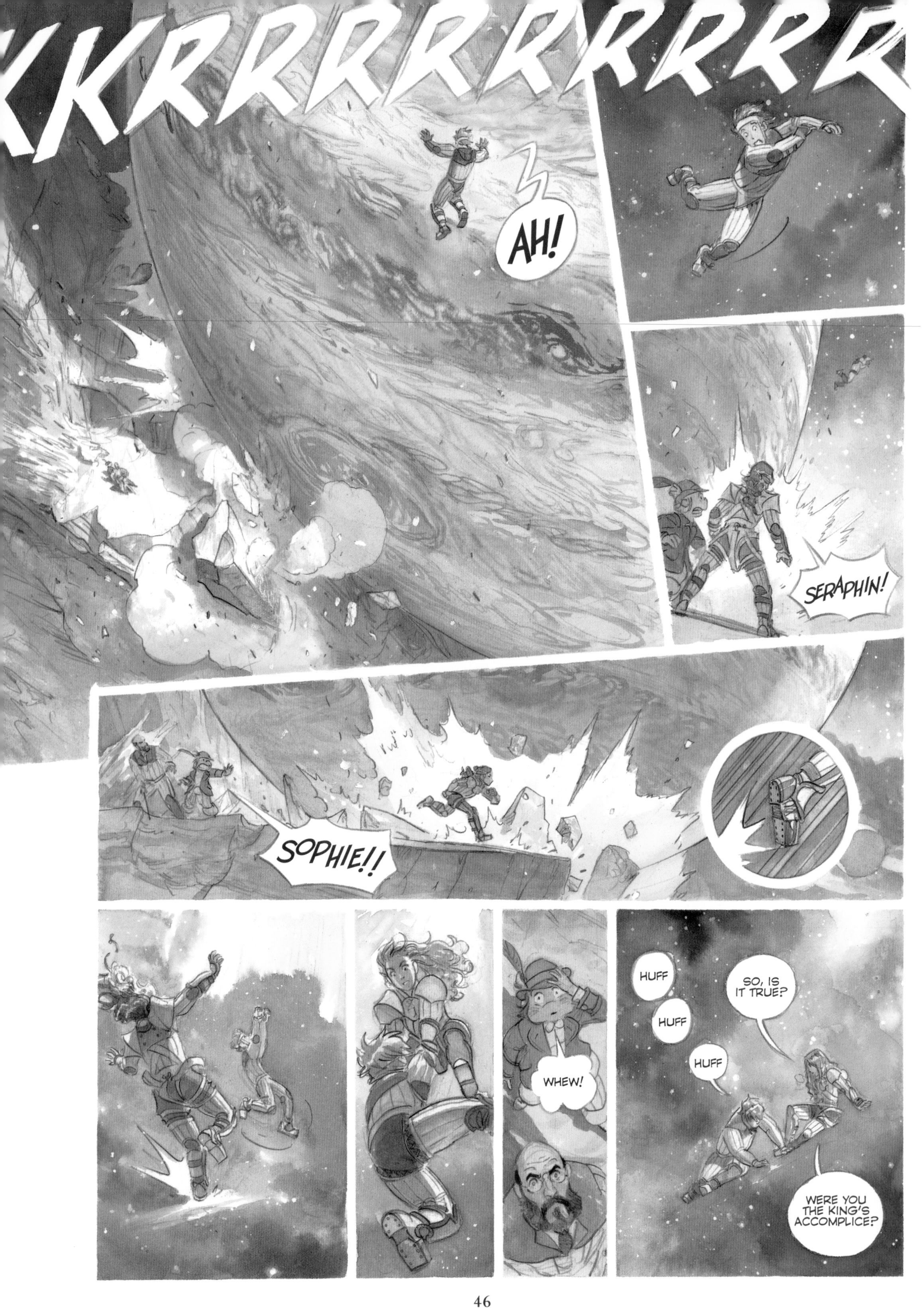
KRRRRRRRRRR
AH!
SERAPHIN!
SOPHIE!!
WHEW!
HUFF
HUFF
HUFF
SO, IS IT TRUE?
WERE YOU THE KING'S ACCOMPLICE?

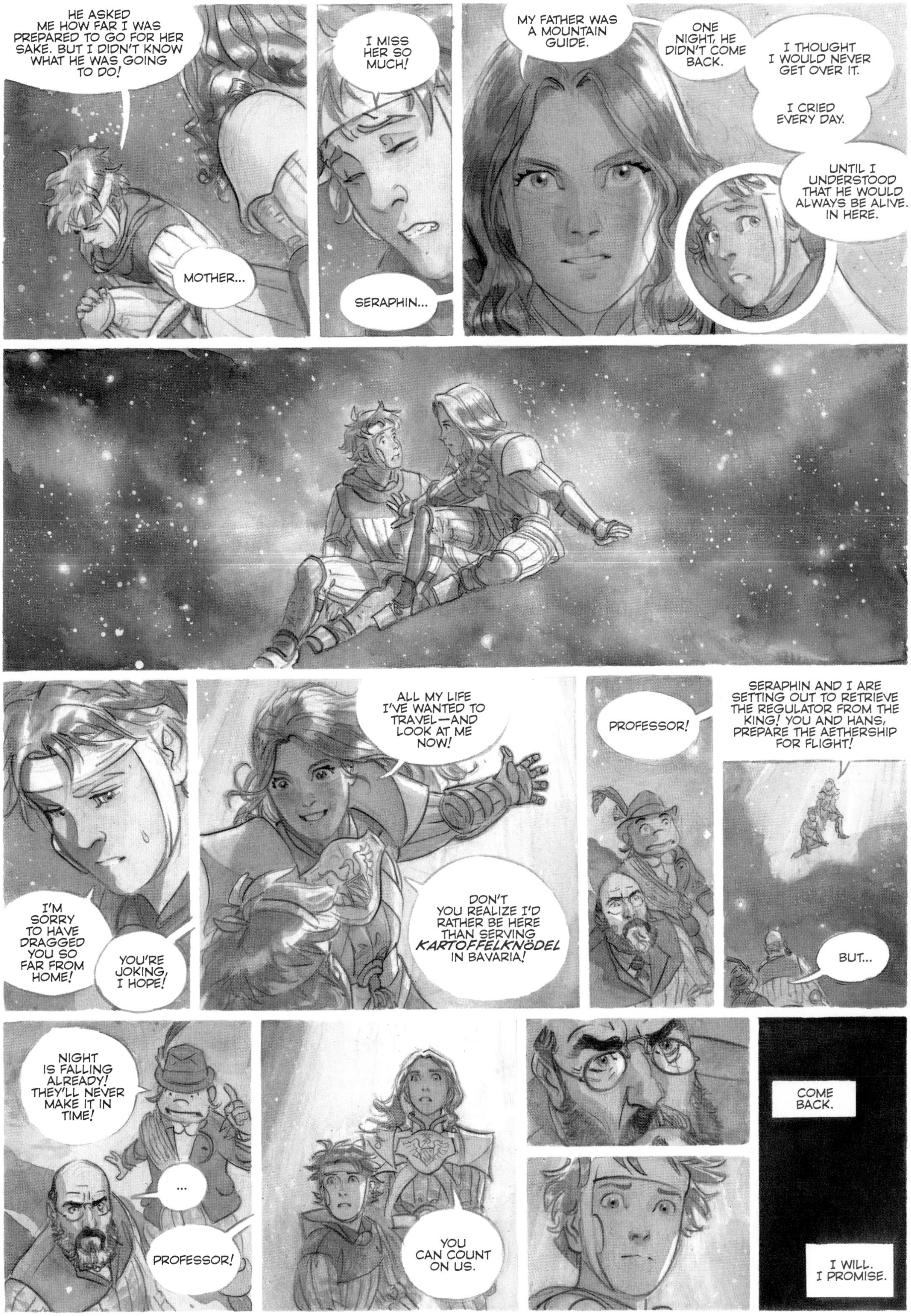

HE ASKED ME HOW FAR I WAS PREPARED TO GO FOR HER SAKE. BUT I DIDN'T KNOW WHAT HE WAS GOING TO DO!
MOTHER...
I MISS HER SO MUCH!
SERAPHIN...
MY FATHER WAS A MOUNTAIN GUIDE.
ONE NIGHT, HE DIDN'T COME BACK.
I THOUGHT I WOULD NEVER GET OVER IT.
I CRIED EVERY DAY.
UNTIL I UNDERSTOOD THAT HE WOULD ALWAYS BE ALIVE. IN HERE.
I'M SORRY TO HAVE DRAGGED YOU SO FAR FROM HOME!
YOU'RE JOKING, I HOPE!
ALL MY LIFE I'VE WANTED TO TRAVEL—AND LOOK AT ME NOW!
DON'T YOU REALIZE I'D RATHER BE HERE THAN SERVING *KARTOFFELKNÖDEL* IN BAVARIA!
PROFESSOR!
SERAPHIN AND I ARE SETTING OUT TO RETRIEVE THE REGULATOR FROM THE KING! YOU AND HANS, PREPARE THE AETHERSHIP FOR FLIGHT!
BUT...
NIGHT IS FALLING ALREADY! THEY'LL NEVER MAKE IT IN TIME!
...
PROFESSOR!
YOU CAN COUNT ON US.
COME BACK.
I WILL. I PROMISE.

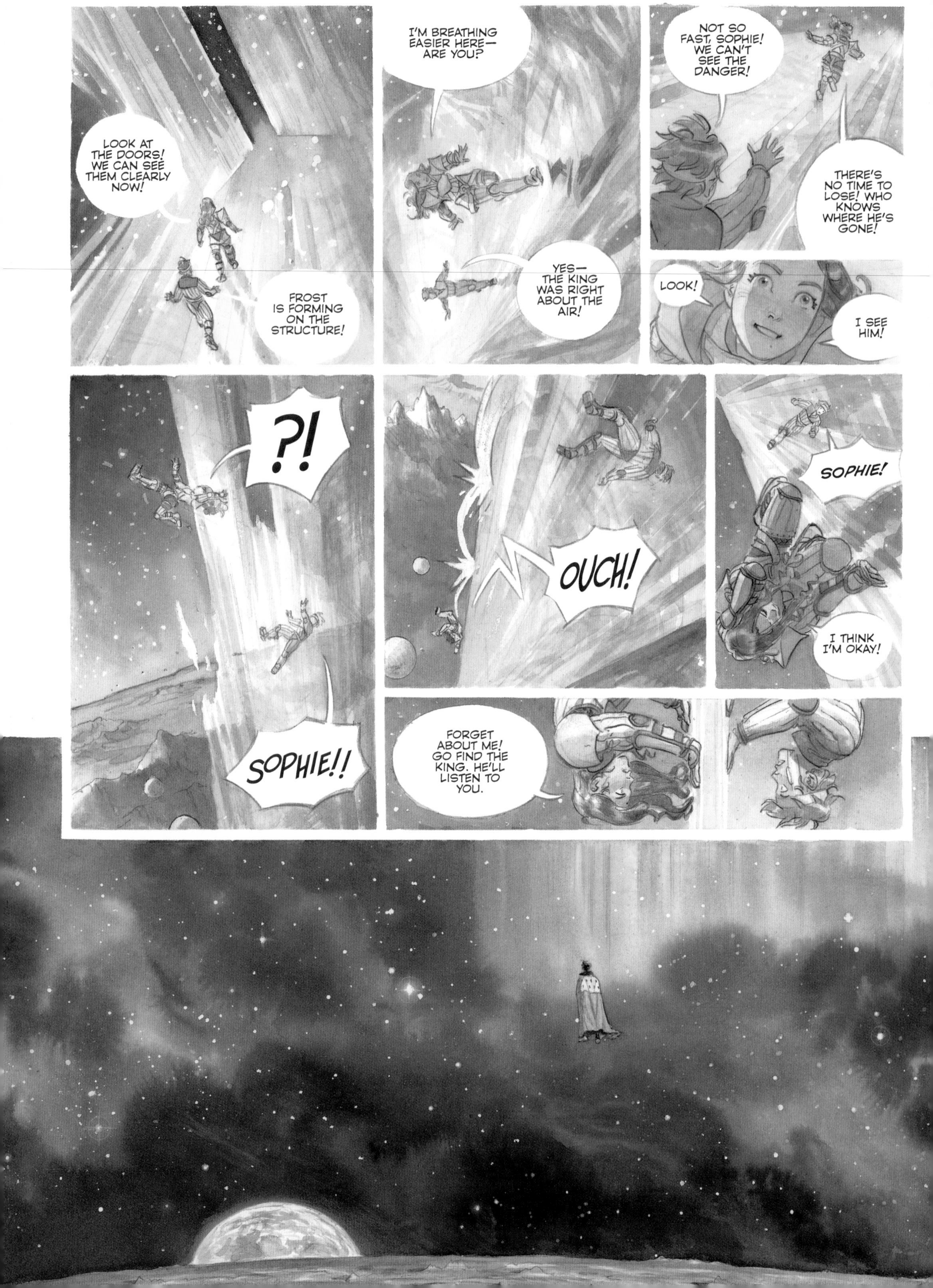
LOOK AT THE DOORS! WE CAN SEE THEM CLEARLY NOW!
FROST IS FORMING ON THE STRUCTURE!
I'M BREATHING EASIER HERE—ARE YOU?
YES—THE KING WAS RIGHT ABOUT THE AIR!
NOT SO FAST, SOPHIE! WE CAN'T SEE THE DANGER!
THERE'S NO TIME TO LOSE! WHO KNOWS WHERE HE'S GONE!
LOOK!
I SEE HIM!
?!
SOPHIE!!
OUCH!
SOPHIE!
I THINK I'M OKAY!
FORGET ABOUT ME! GO FIND THE KING. HE'LL LISTEN TO YOU.

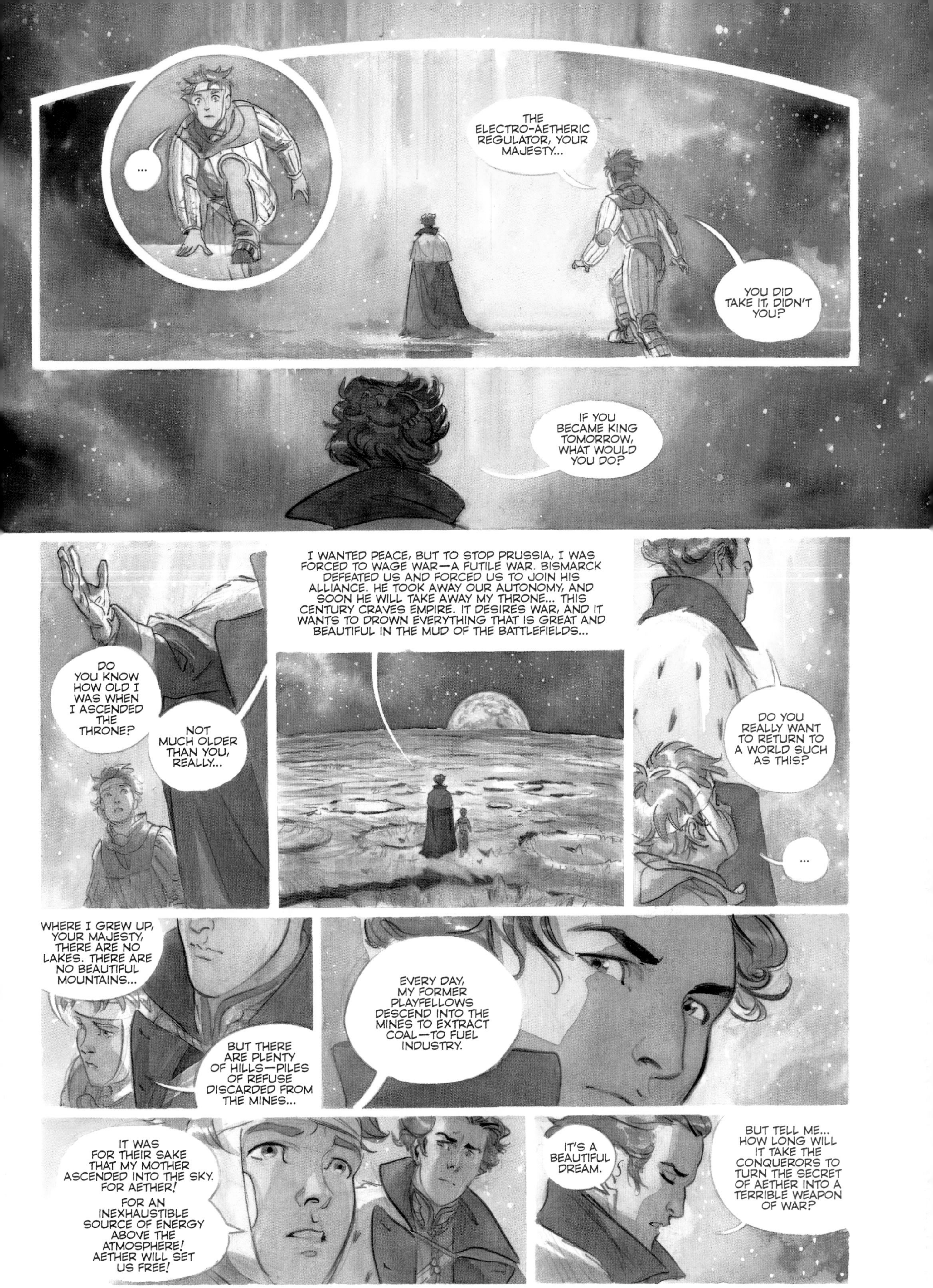
...
THE ELECTRO-AETHERIC REGULATOR, YOUR MAJESTY...
YOU DID TAKE IT, DIDN'T YOU?
IF YOU BECAME KING TOMORROW, WHAT WOULD YOU DO?
DO YOU KNOW HOW OLD I WAS WHEN I ASCENDED THE THRONE?
NOT MUCH OLDER THAN YOU, REALLY...
I WANTED PEACE, BUT TO STOP PRUSSIA, I WAS FORCED TO WAGE WAR—A FUTILE WAR. BISMARCK DEFEATED US AND FORCED US TO JOIN HIS ALLIANCE. HE TOOK AWAY OUR AUTONOMY, AND SOON HE WILL TAKE AWAY MY THRONE... THIS CENTURY CRAVES EMPIRE. IT DESIRES WAR, AND IT WANTS TO DROWN EVERYTHING THAT IS GREAT AND BEAUTIFUL IN THE MUD OF THE BATTLEFIELDS...
DO YOU REALLY WANT TO RETURN TO A WORLD SUCH AS THIS?
...
WHERE I GREW UP, YOUR MAJESTY, THERE ARE NO LAKES. THERE ARE NO BEAUTIFUL MOUNTAINS...
BUT THERE ARE PLENTY OF HILLS—PILES OF REFUSE DISCARDED FROM THE MINES...
EVERY DAY, MY FORMER PLAYFELLOWS DESCEND INTO THE MINES TO EXTRACT COAL—TO FUEL INDUSTRY.
IT WAS FOR THEIR SAKE THAT MY MOTHER ASCENDED INTO THE SKY. FOR AETHER!
FOR AN INEXHAUSTIBLE SOURCE OF ENERGY ABOVE THE ATMOSPHERE! AETHER WILL SET US FREE!
IT'S A BEAUTIFUL DREAM.
BUT TELL ME... HOW LONG WILL IT TAKE THE CONQUERORS TO TURN THE SECRET OF AETHER INTO A TERRIBLE WEAPON OF WAR?

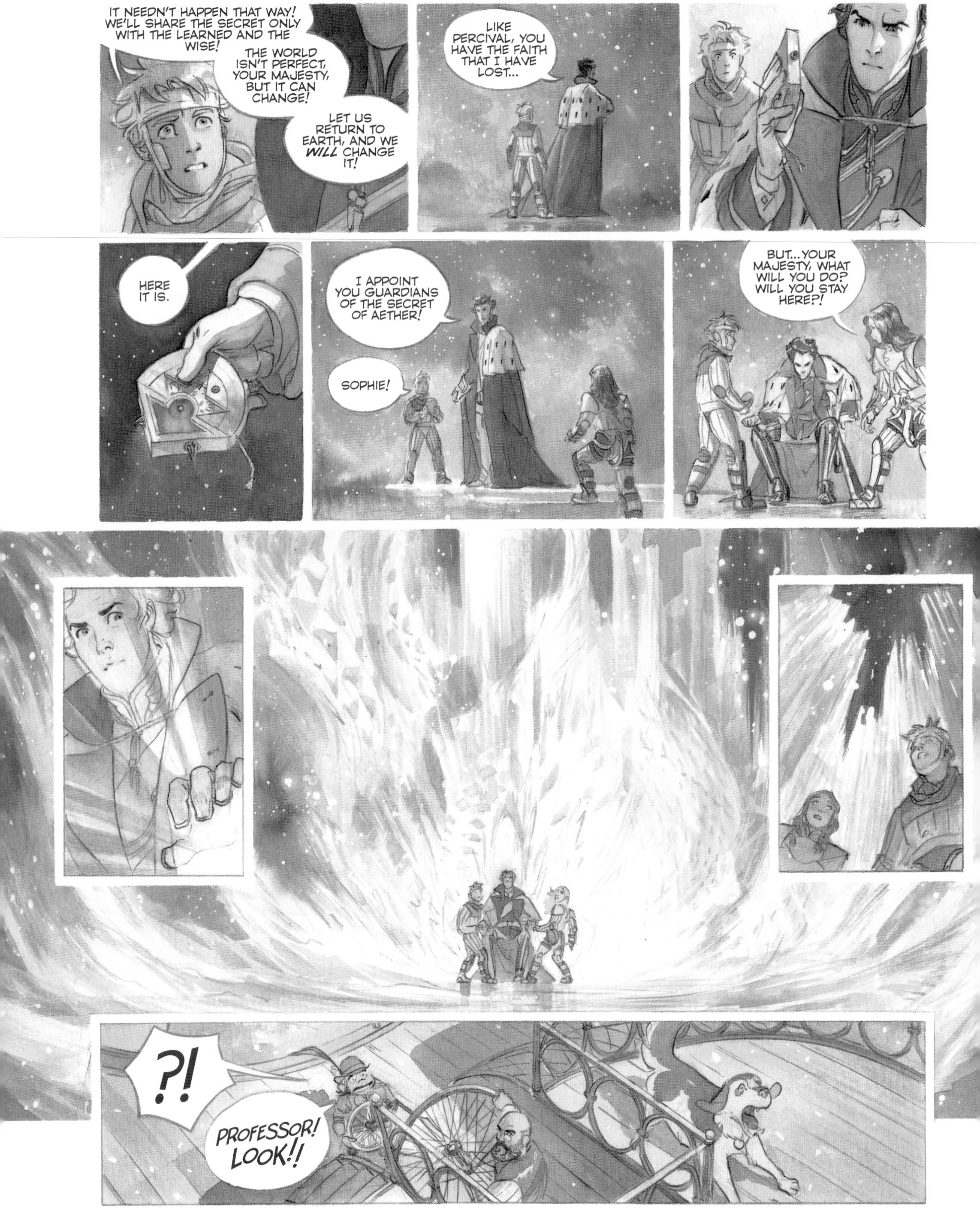
IT NEEDN'T HAPPEN THAT WAY! WE'LL SHARE THE SECRET ONLY WITH THE LEARNED AND THE WISE!
THE WORLD ISN'T PERFECT, YOUR MAJESTY, BUT IT CAN CHANGE!
LET US RETURN TO EARTH, AND WE WILL CHANGE IT!
LIKE PERCIVAL, YOU HAVE THE FAITH THAT I HAVE LOST...
HERE IT IS.
I APPOINT YOU GUARDIANS OF THE SECRET OF AETHER!
SOPHIE!
BUT...YOUR MAJESTY, WHAT WILL YOU DO? WILL YOU STAY HERE?!
?!
PROFESSOR! LOOK!!

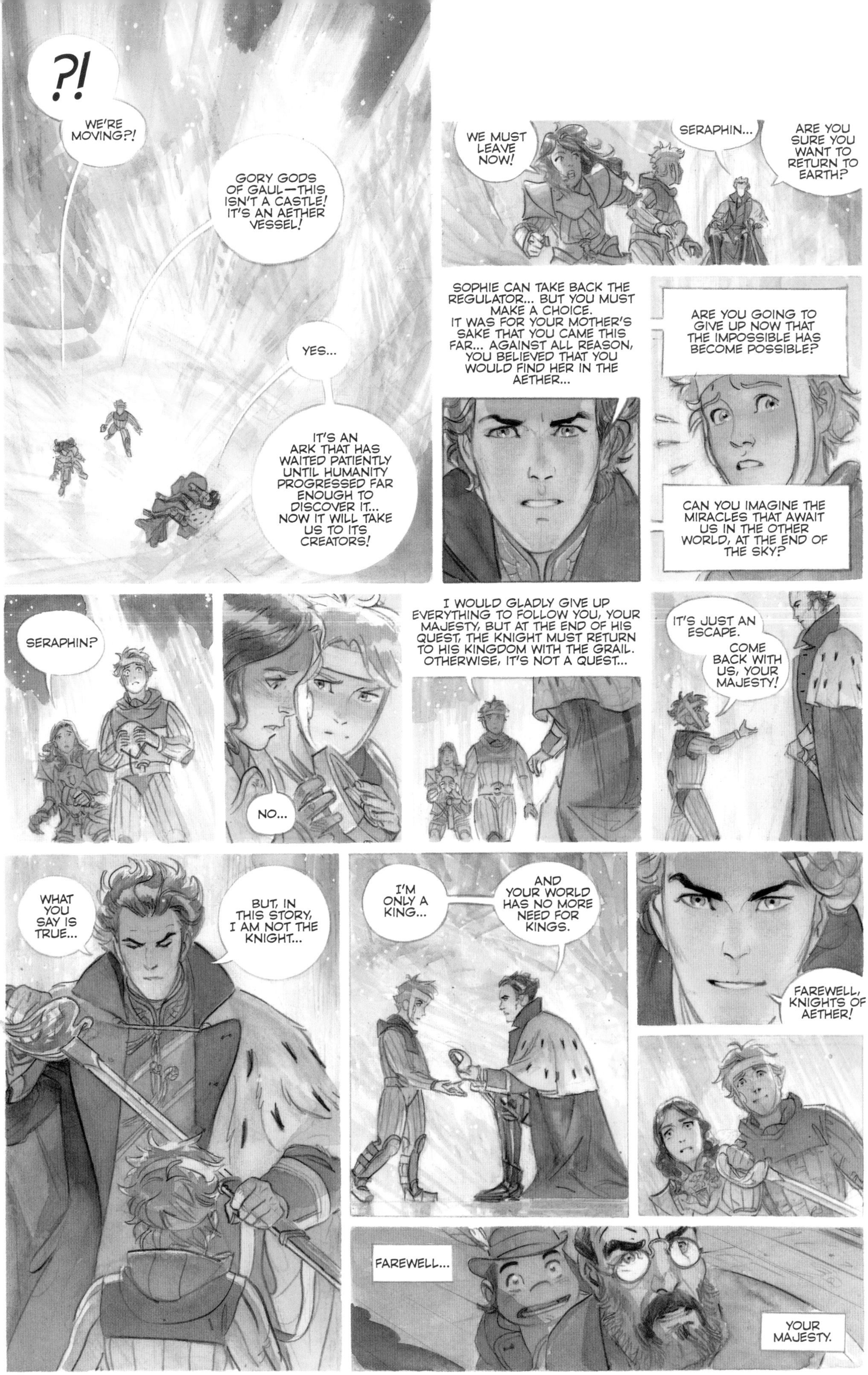
?!
WE'RE MOVING?!
GORY GODS OF GAUL—THIS ISN'T A CASTLE! IT'S AN AETHER VESSEL!
YES...
IT'S AN ARK THAT HAS WAITED PATIENTLY UNTIL HUMANITY PROGRESSED FAR ENOUGH TO DISCOVER IT... NOW IT WILL TAKE US TO ITS CREATORS!
WE MUST LEAVE NOW!
SERAPHIN...
ARE YOU SURE YOU WANT TO RETURN TO EARTH?
SOPHIE CAN TAKE BACK THE REGULATOR... BUT YOU MUST MAKE A CHOICE.
IT WAS FOR YOUR MOTHER'S SAKE THAT YOU CAME THIS FAR... AGAINST ALL REASON, YOU BELIEVED THAT YOU WOULD FIND HER IN THE AETHER...
ARE YOU GOING TO GIVE UP NOW THAT THE IMPOSSIBLE HAS BECOME POSSIBLE?
CAN YOU IMAGINE THE MIRACLES THAT AWAIT US IN THE OTHER WORLD, AT THE END OF THE SKY?
SERAPHIN?
NO...
I WOULD GLADLY GIVE UP EVERYTHING TO FOLLOW YOU, YOUR MAJESTY, BUT AT THE END OF HIS QUEST, THE KNIGHT MUST RETURN TO HIS KINGDOM WITH THE GRAIL. OTHERWISE, IT'S NOT A QUEST...
IT'S JUST AN ESCAPE.
COME BACK WITH US, YOUR MAJESTY!
WHAT YOU SAY IS TRUE...
BUT, IN THIS STORY, I AM NOT THE KNIGHT...
I'M ONLY A KING...
AND YOUR WORLD HAS NO MORE NEED FOR KINGS.
FAREWELL, KNIGHTS OF AETHER!
FAREWELL...
YOUR MAJESTY.

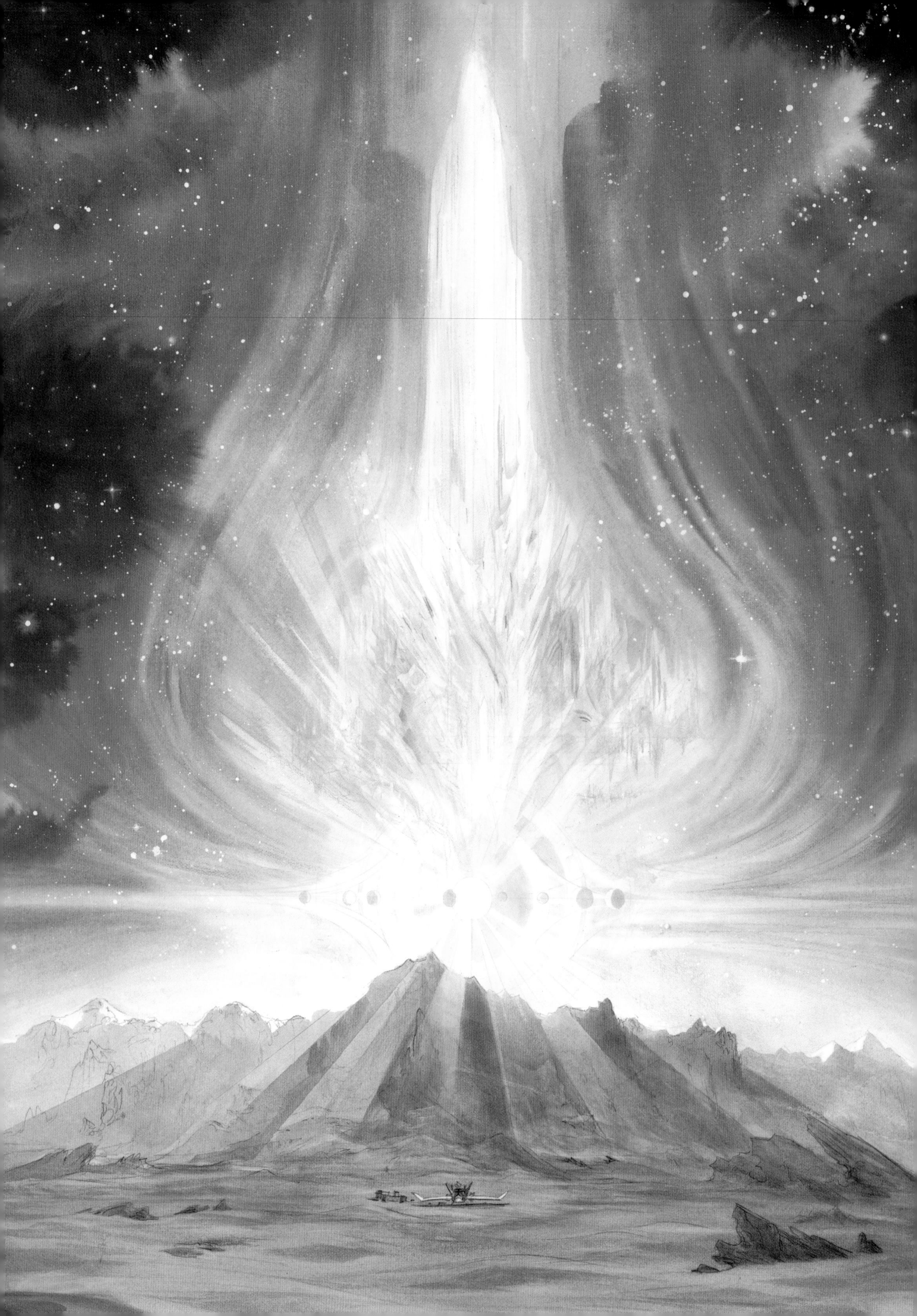

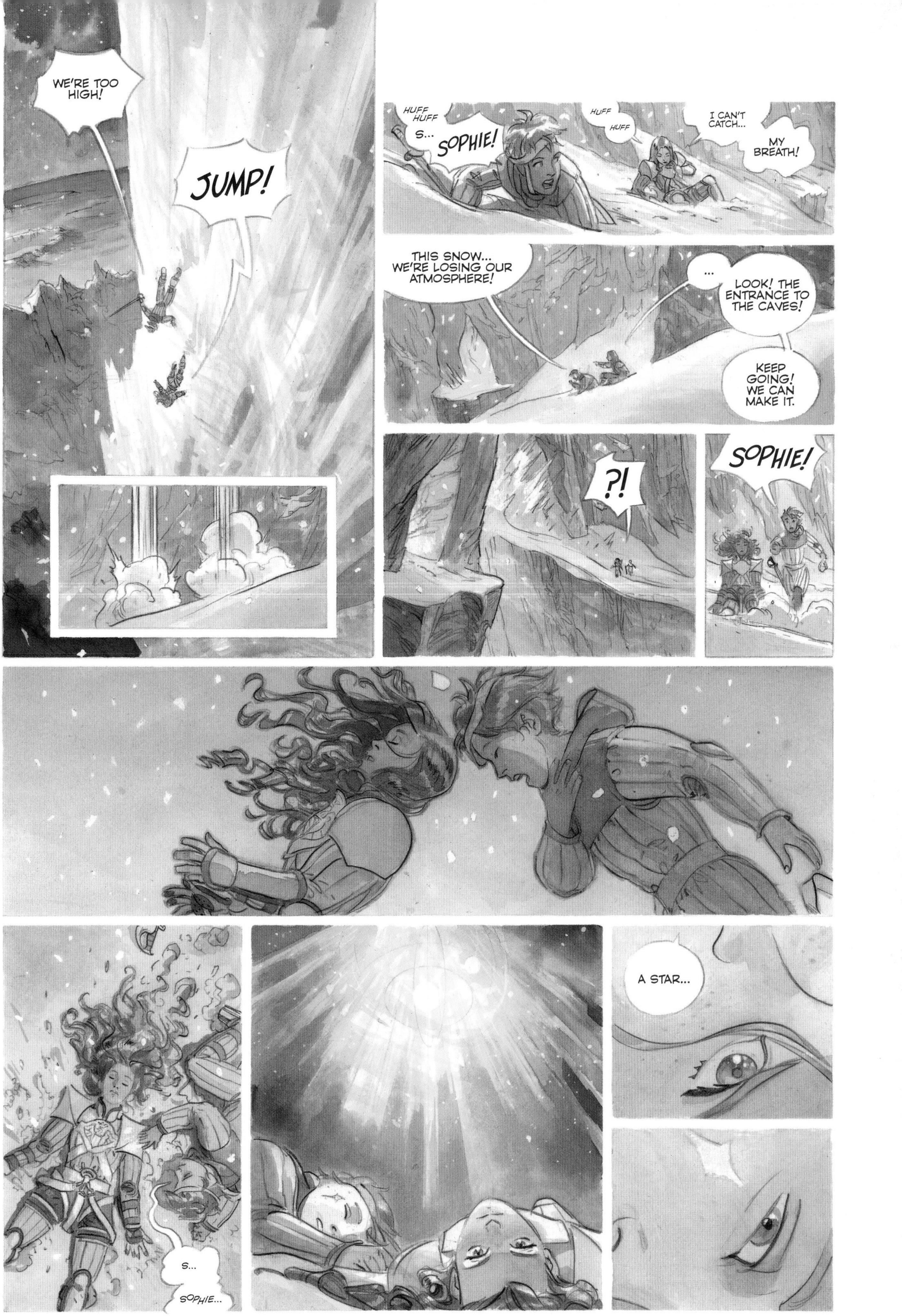
WE'RE TOO HIGH!
JUMP!
HUFF HUFF
S... SOPHIE!
HUFF
HUFF
I CAN'T CATCH...
MY BREATH!
THIS SNOW... WE'RE LOSING OUR ATMOSPHERE!
...
LOOK! THE ENTRANCE TO THE CAVES!
KEEP GOING! WE CAN MAKE IT.
?!
SOPHIE!
S...
SOPHIE...
A STAR...

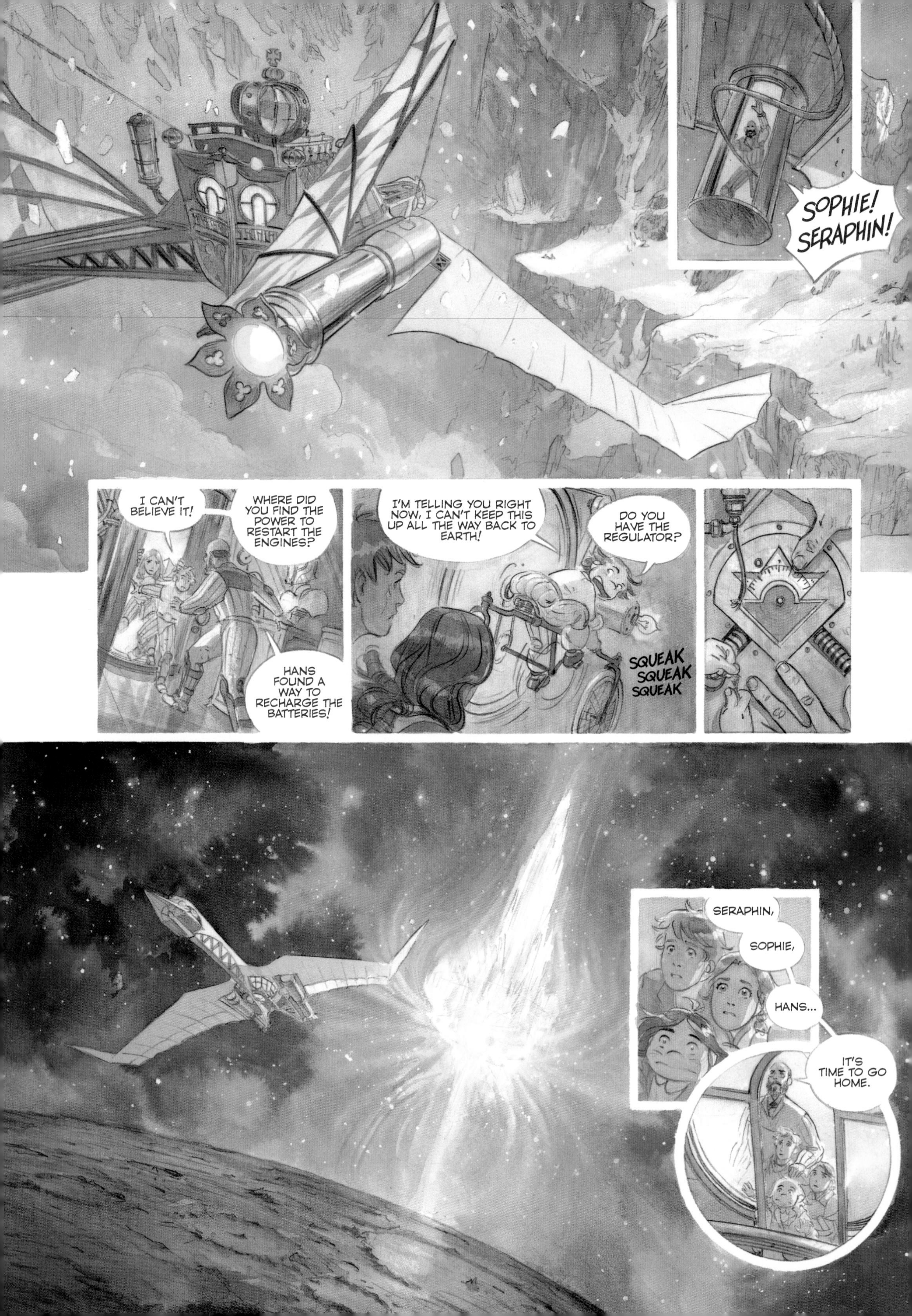
SOPHIE! SERAPHIN!
I CAN'T BELIEVE IT!
WHERE DID YOU FIND THE POWER TO RESTART THE ENGINES?
HANS FOUND A WAY TO RECHARGE THE BATTERIES!
I'M TELLING YOU RIGHT NOW, I CAN'T KEEP THIS UP ALL THE WAY BACK TO EARTH!
DO YOU HAVE THE REGULATOR?
SQUEAK SQUEAK SQUEAK
SERAPHIN,
SOPHIE,
HANS...
IT'S TIME TO GO HOME.

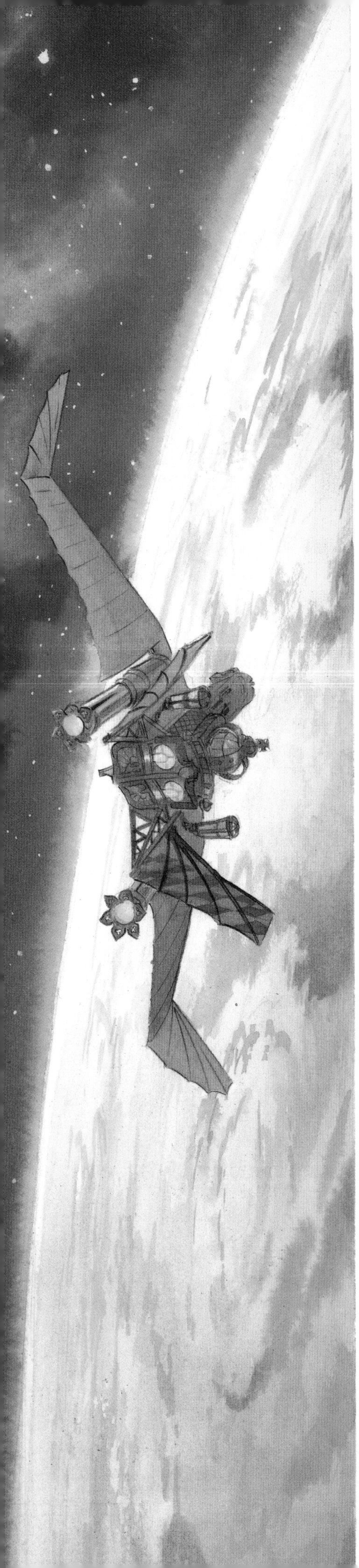

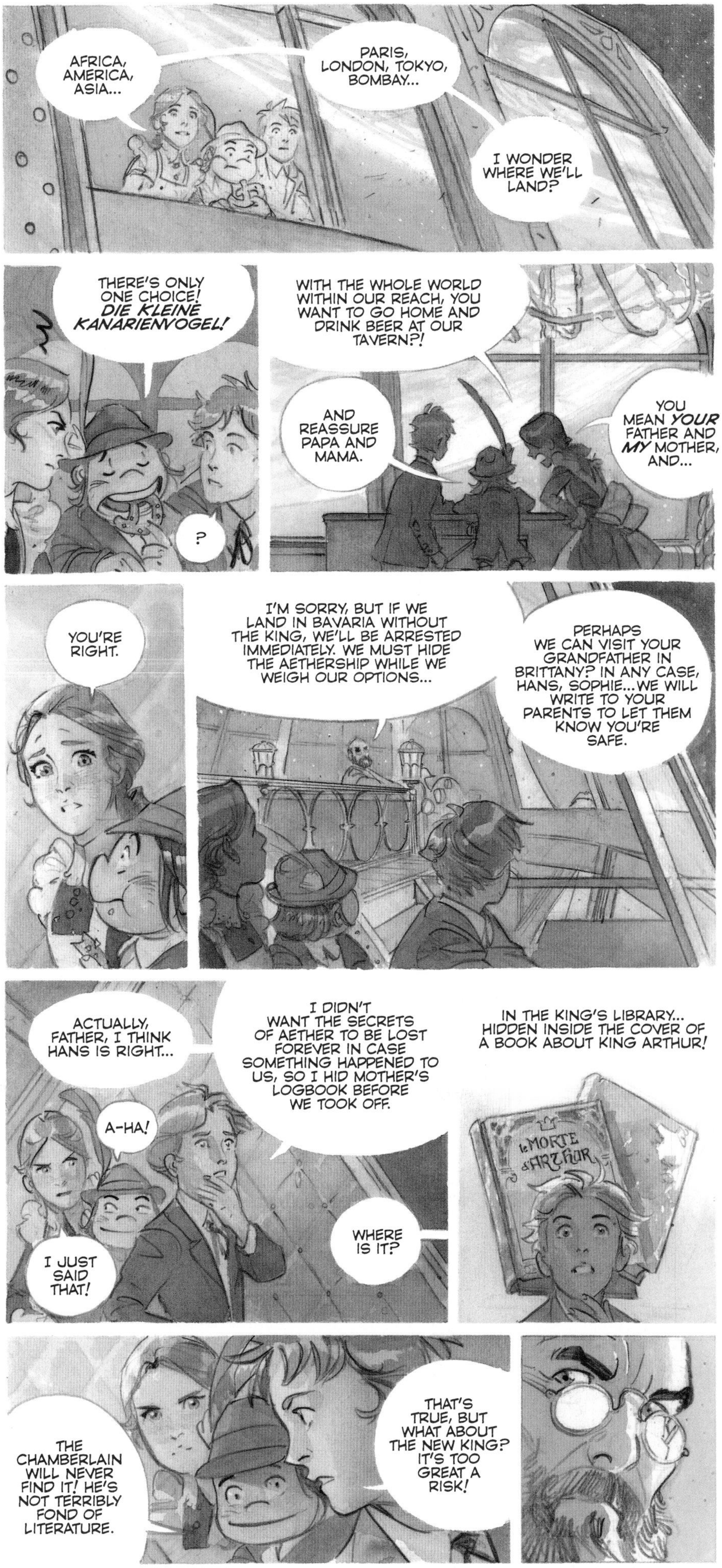
AFRICA, AMERICA, ASIA...
PARIS, LONDON, TOKYO, BOMBAY...
I WONDER WHERE WE'LL LAND?
THERE'S ONLY ONE CHOICE! *DIE KLEINE KANARIENVOGEL!*
?
WITH THE WHOLE WORLD WITHIN OUR REACH, YOU WANT TO GO HOME AND DRINK BEER AT OUR TAVERN?!
AND REASSURE PAPA AND MAMA.
YOU MEAN ***YOUR*** FATHER AND ***MY*** MOTHER, AND...
YOU'RE RIGHT.
I'M SORRY, BUT IF WE LAND IN BAVARIA WITHOUT THE KING, WE'LL BE ARRESTED IMMEDIATELY. WE MUST HIDE THE AETHERSHIP WHILE WE WEIGH OUR OPTIONS...
PERHAPS WE CAN VISIT YOUR GRANDFATHER IN BRITTANY? IN ANY CASE, HANS, SOPHIE... WE WILL WRITE TO YOUR PARENTS TO LET THEM KNOW YOU'RE SAFE.
ACTUALLY, FATHER, I THINK HANS IS RIGHT...
A-HA!
I JUST SAID THAT!
I DIDN'T WANT THE SECRETS OF AETHER TO BE LOST FOREVER IN CASE SOMETHING HAPPENED TO US, SO I HID MOTHER'S LOGBOOK BEFORE WE TOOK OFF.
WHERE IS IT?
IN THE KING'S LIBRARY... HIDDEN INSIDE THE COVER OF A BOOK ABOUT KING ARTHUR!
THE CHAMBERLAIN WILL NEVER FIND IT! HE'S NOT TERRIBLY FOND OF LITERATURE.
THAT'S TRUE, BUT WHAT ABOUT THE NEW KING? IT'S TOO GREAT A RISK!

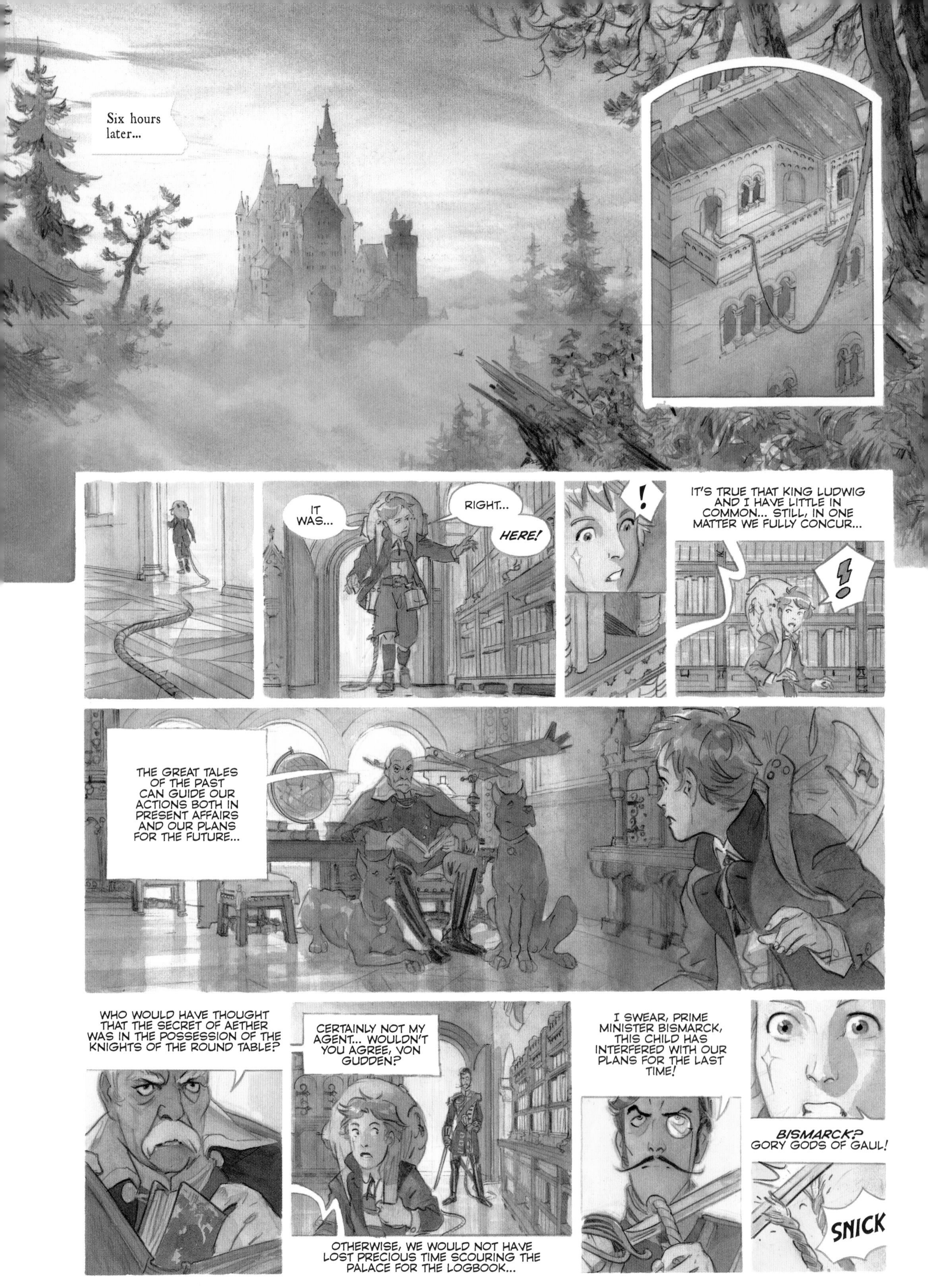

Six hours later...
IT WAS...
RIGHT...
HERE!
!
IT'S TRUE THAT KING LUDWIG AND I HAVE LITTLE IN COMMON... STILL, IN ONE MATTER WE FULLY CONCUR...
!
THE GREAT TALES OF THE PAST CAN GUIDE OUR ACTIONS BOTH IN PRESENT AFFAIRS AND OUR PLANS FOR THE FUTURE...
WHO WOULD HAVE THOUGHT THAT THE SECRET OF AETHER WAS IN THE POSSESSION OF THE KNIGHTS OF THE ROUND TABLE?
CERTAINLY NOT MY AGENT... WOULDN'T YOU AGREE, VON GUDDEN?
OTHERWISE, WE WOULD NOT HAVE LOST PRECIOUS TIME SCOURING THE PALACE FOR THE LOGBOOK...
I SWEAR, PRIME MINISTER BISMARCK, THIS CHILD HAS INTERFERED WITH OUR PLANS FOR THE LAST TIME!
BISMARCK? GORY GODS OF GAUL!
SNICK

PROFESSOR DULAC, I PRESUME...

!?

AT LAST, I MEET THE INVENTOR OF THE AETHER ENGINE... I AM HONORED.

I READ YOUR WIFE'S LOGBOOK. SHE WAS, BEYOND DOUBT, A TRULY REMARKABLE WOMAN...

IT IS UNFORTUNATE THAT FRANCE REFUSED TO ACKNOWLEDGE HER DISCOVERIES...

BUT PRUSSIA STANDS READY TO HONOR HER MEMORY AND REWARD YOUR GENIUS.

YOUR CRAFT IS FIRMLY SECURED.

PLEASE COME DOWN AND JOIN US, SO THAT WE CAN CONTINUE OUR DISCUSSION IN GREATER COMFORT.

FATHER, NO!

WE MUST PROTECT THE SECRET OF AETHER!

TOO LATE, BRAT! YOUR SECRET'S OUT!

OW!

FATHER! DON'T LET THEM CAPTURE YOU!!

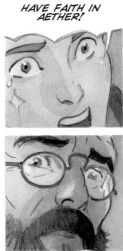

HAVE FAITH IN AETHER!

?!

YOU SURPRISE ME, PROFESSOR. I'VE ALWAYS RESPECTED YOUR INTEGRITY...

BUT I NEVER THOUGHT YOU'D ABANDON YOUR FAMILY...

SCHWEINHUND!

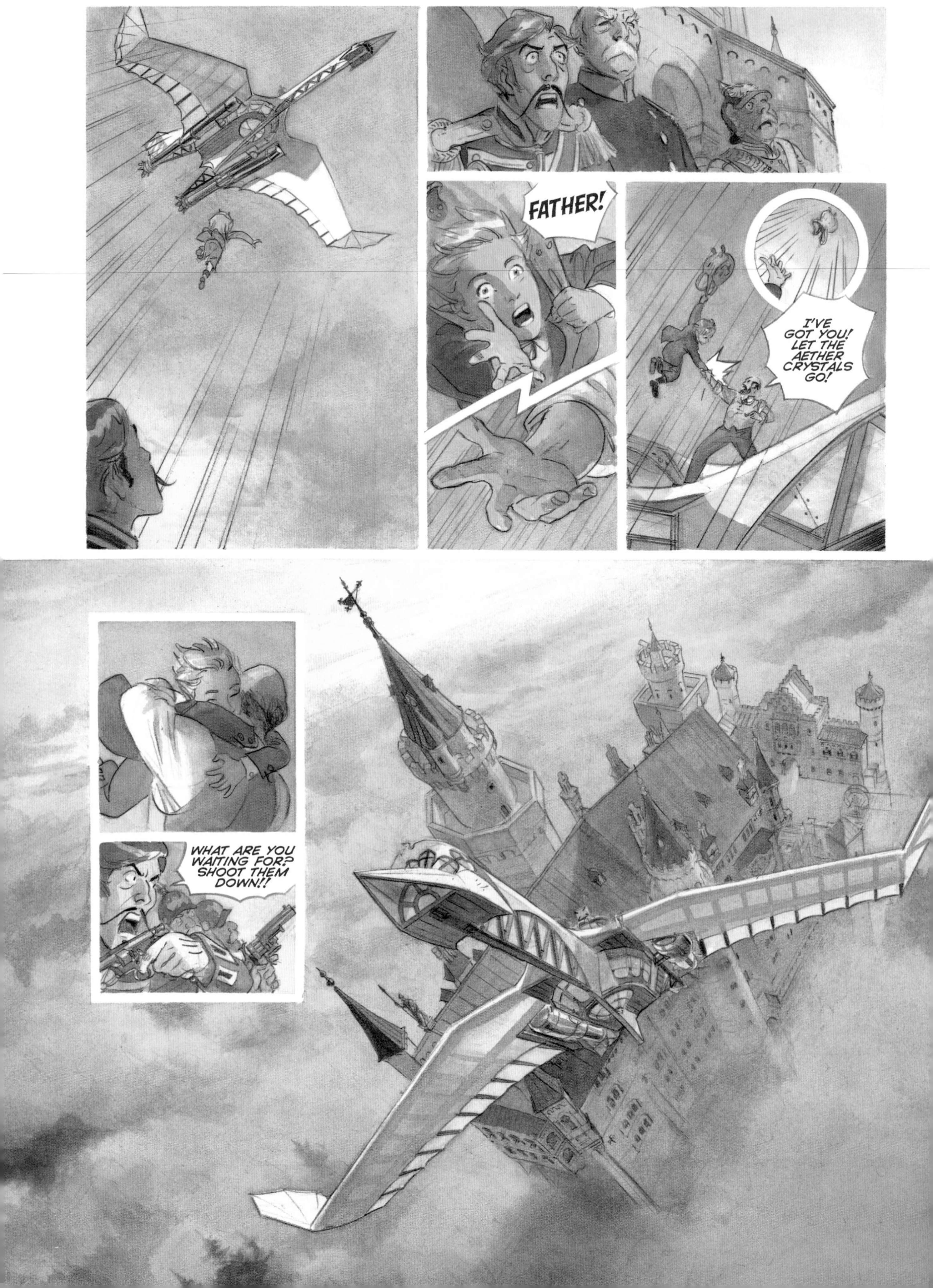
FATHER!
I'VE GOT YOU! LET THE AETHER CRYSTALS GO!
WHAT ARE YOU WAITING FOR? SHOOT THEM DOWN!!

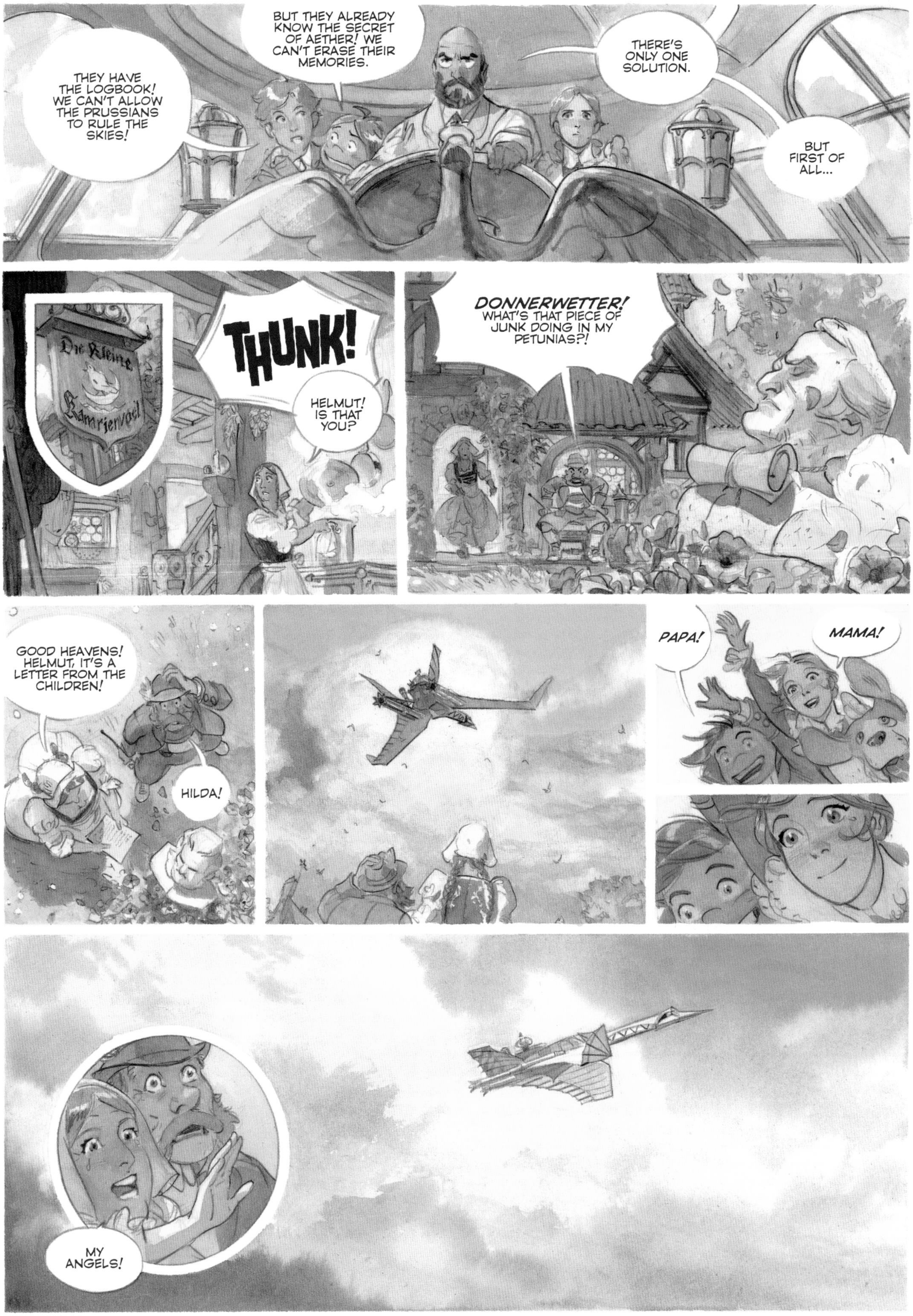
THEY HAVE THE LOGBOOK! WE CAN'T ALLOW THE PRUSSIANS TO RULE THE SKIES!
BUT THEY ALREADY KNOW THE SECRET OF AETHER! WE CAN'T ERASE THEIR MEMORIES.
THERE'S ONLY ONE SOLUTION.
BUT FIRST OF ALL...
Die Kleine Kanarienvogel
THUNK!
HELMUT! IS THAT YOU?
DONNERWETTER! WHAT'S THAT PIECE OF JUNK DOING IN MY PETUNIAS?!
GOOD HEAVENS! HELMUT, IT'S A LETTER FROM THE CHILDREN!
HILDA!
PAPA!
MAMA!
MY ANGELS!

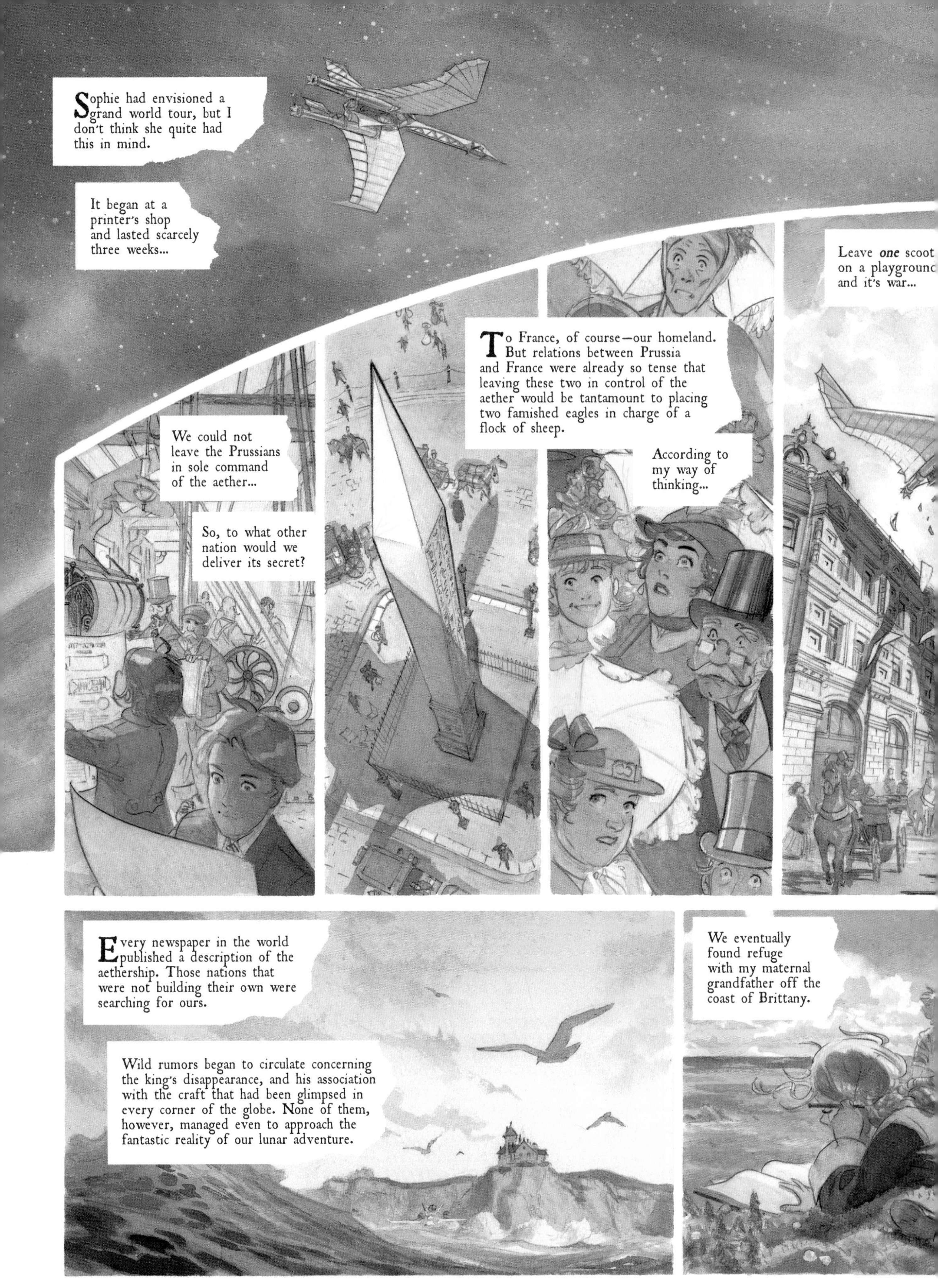
Sophie had envisioned a grand world tour, but I don't think she quite had this in mind.
It began at a printer's shop and lasted scarcely three weeks...
We could not leave the Prussians in sole command of the aether...
So, to what other nation would we deliver its secret?
To France, of course—our homeland. But relations between Prussia and France were already so tense that leaving these two in control of the aether would be tantamount to placing two famished eagles in charge of a flock of sheep.
According to my way of thinking...
Leave *one* scoot on a playgrounc and it's war...
Every newspaper in the world published a description of the aethership. Those nations that were not building their own were searching for ours.
Wild rumors began to circulate concerning the king's disappearance, and his association with the craft that had been glimpsed in every corner of the globe. None of them, however, managed even to approach the fantastic reality of our lunar adventure.
We eventually found refuge with my maternal grandfather off the coast of Brittany.